Other Books by
Columbus Creative Cooperative

For the Road

Short Stories of America's Highways

Edited By
Emily Hitchcock & Brad Pauquette

Proudly Presented By

Pauquette ltd
dba Columbus Creative Cooperative
PO Box 91028
Columbus, OH 43209
www.ColumbusCoop.org

Cover Artwork by Michelle Berki

Design and Production by
Columbus Publishing Lab
www.ColumbusPublishingLab.com

Print ISBN 978-1-63337-017-3
Ebook ISBN 978-1-63337-018-0

Printed in the United States of America
1 3 5 7 9 10 8 6 4 2

CONTENTS

To those who take the road less traveled.

INTRODUCTION

A merica has a great literary tradition of the road. From Steinbeck's *Travels with Charley* and *The Grapes of Wrath*, to Kerouac's *On the Road* or McCarthy's *The Road*, the highway has consistently represented a place of adventure and the prospect of something better over the horizon.

When we put out a call for submissions along the theme "Modern American Highways," I expected to receive stories of hitchhiking from coast to coast, drifters with hearts of gold, migrant workers in search of a better life. Instead, I learned something about the modern perception of the road—we're terrified of it.

Most of all, we're terrified of strangers in the night. We're terrified of what lies in wait in the darkness when we're alone, secured only by the illusion of voice-activated emergency distress calls.

In fairness, the road is legitimately fearsome. Every day, in cities and rural highways across the country, nearly 100 people die violent, brutal deaths at the hands of their automobiles, their bodies pulverized between plates of steel, their heads crushed through windshields, and their chests impaled by steering wheel columns. Don't forget about being burned alive. For Americans between the ages of five and thirty-four, motor vehicle fatalities are the leading cause of death.

But that's not why we're afraid. It's interesting to me that we'll adjust our lifestyle to accommodate all kinds of risk—we'll only smoke at parties, or only drink alcohol on the weekends to reduce our risk of cancer and other lifestyle ailments. We'll hire a roofing company for the second story

1

because we don't have the right safety gear. We'll spend twice as much on food to limit GMOs and pesticides, to avoid some probable but unnamed illness that we're certain these things are responsible for. We'll encourage our young adults to practice "safe sex." But no one ever limits their time in a motor vehicle in order to reduce the risk of fatality.

No, we're not afraid of the road because these death machines we call cars might mangle our bodies and leave us to bleed out alone in a ditch alongside of a deserted roadway.

We're afraid of the imaginary people we have created, as a society, to walk the long stretch of road through the hot sun and into the night, felons and deviants we've invented to stalk and threaten and destroy.

Your risk of dying or being sexually assaulted in a hitchhiking related incident is literally less than one in a million. Perhaps we've invented these ludicrous dangers *outside* of the vehicle in order to insulate our psyches from the very real dangers *inside* of the car. We're behaving safely, we tell ourselves, because we didn't pick up an escaped convict along the side of the road, all the while we're hurtling headfirst down the roadway in a tin can with brake pads manufactured by the lowest bidder.

Many of the stories in this book will prey on your fears. They'll take hold of the fear constructs we've installed as a society, and reinforce and twist these imaginary dangers deeper into your mind.

But, in good conscience, I need to tell you…we're fucking with you. You're more likely to meet your future spouse, business partner or a new best friend than get stabbed while traveling the open road.

There's a beautiful America out there, full of wonderful people. Enjoy these stories, be convinced by them even, but don't let us scare you away from our fantastic highways.

-Brad Pauquette

GOING SOUTH

Noell Wolfgram Evans

O n the day this all started, I'm not sure what the impetus was but the spirit moved me and I decided that if the duck was still there, I'd offer him a ride. As I rolled up to the corner, there he was, right between the fire hydrant and the "Slow Kids" sign. Rolling down the car window just a little, I asked, "Is everything okay?"

The duck just stood there, looking completely disinterested, which of course only piqued *my* interest. I reached across the front seat and opened the car door. "Hey," I shouted, "you need a ride or something?"

Even though I *had* asked, I was still surprised when he nodded nervously and climbed into the passenger seat. He struggled a little with the seatbelt but finally he was ready. There we were, and as he started playing with the automatic windows I realized that I had no idea what to do next. Where did this duck want to go? He was either unable or uninterested in telling me so I just started driving.

When I picked him up, I knew that I would be playing with fire.

After all, he had the *Fire* board game tucked under his wing. I understood that there was a certain danger involved in picking up a hitchhiker, but strangely enough, I didn't care. Just once I wanted to live on the edge, to do something bold, to prove to myself I still had something left, and if this hitchhiking duck ended up chopping me to pieces with a chainsaw, well I will have gone out leaving my mark *and* giving my grandma an opportunity to tell everyone she had warned me this would happen.

I looked over at the duck and realized that he wasn't wearing any pants. I blushed a little at the awkwardness of the situation. Turning back to the road (while hoping that the duck hadn't noticed me staring) I wondered if the duck had a family. Was he running to them? Or from them? Were they out in the streets, checking hospitals, scouring apartment complex ponds, and flying across other places that ducks go in hopes of finding him and convincing him to come home? Or was he, like me, in need of a change? Was *he* seeking an adventure too? Suddenly I knew—south. This duck was trying to get south. I had seen enough cartoons to know that ducks went south. They fly down there, tag some statue or something and then fly back north. It's what's known as the Circle of Life.

The most spontaneous and dangerous thing I had done up to this point was, once, at the doctor's office I was reading a *Glamour* magazine and I enjoyed a story so much that I ripped it out, right there in the waiting room. I started to get that same tingly feeling—I was going to do this. I was going to drive this duck south.

I announced this to the duck who looked at me somewhat blankly, overcome I am sure with gratitude and emotion. Since I wasn't sure what part of the south ducks were supposed to go to, I figured I would take him in a general southerly direction and we would just watch for other ducks.

As we drove past semis hauling cars, tour buses hauling seniors, and those large circular trucks hauling the mystery liquid ("Not For Human

Consumption"), the duck and I put a hand and a wing out the window and did the swimming through the air thing. I could imagine the thoughts of the people who passed us—jealous men seeing their adventurous childhood dreams played out, bored housewives placing themselves into a fantasy of escape, and young children looking on slack-jawed proclaiming: "That dude is hanging out with a duck!" I drove a little faster.

About three hours into the trip, due in part to his stoic, silent nature, I started to consider the possibility that this duck was actually the physical form of an omnipotent being. Perhaps my picking up this stranded traveler was some cosmic test. Conversely, I understood that it was not outside the realm of possibility that I was just an idiot being taken advantage of by a lazy duck.

I remarked that this seemed like a scene in a movie, to which he shuddered in a way that said, "Movies are mindless wastes of mental capacity and hardly a step forward in the quest to achieve a greater consciousness with one's true-self and the universe as it exists in its pure form. True art, that which offers aesthetic, emotional, psychological, and mental engagement and growth, can only be found in one form—literature. Particularly in the works of Halfdan Rasmussen."

I felt stupid. I turned all of my attention to the white lines that were rolling under the car. I know that you're supposed to drive *between* the lines, but I've always found a certain comfort in driving *over* them, pretending my car is Pac-Man.

We had just completed our first "comfort break" when I began to assess where we were in the drive, and in our relationship. I felt like neither was going all that well. We were having a hard time getting on the same wavelength. I wanted to talk about baseball, he wanted to talk about fish; I brought up *Star Wars*, he brought up fish; I tried cards, but he brought it back to fish. He did mention that he had just finished refurbishing a 4-Jet carburetor on a 1957 Chevy 283 Rochester Bel Air 4-Barrel; I had nothing.

Unconsciously, my hand reached to the radio and started working through the stations. It knew better than I that a little traveling music might lessen the pressure to engage. The hard part—what kind of music would a duck like? (I realized that by considering such a blanket question I was putting a stereotype on him and I made a mental note to make some sort of reparation to the Duck Awareness Fund.) Running the options through my head of what was available, I remembered that I had the Kenny Rogers CD *21 Number Ones*. I figured, everyone loves Kenny, and I was right!

Kenny sang as we moved past one farm that seamlessly became another. The sun was coming down with splintered rays that reached through the clouds like the fingers of God. In the front yard of one particular farmhouse a child swung on a tire swing, and I thought to myself, this must be where they film all those commercials about America.

"On a warm summer's eve. On a train bound for nowhere…"

At this most American of moments Kenny started *"The Gambler"* but he only got two lines in before the CD jumped to the next track. I looked at the CD player to see what was going on when I saw the duck's wing recoiling.

"Did you just skip 'The Gambler'?"

After a moment, he spoke: "Quack!"

Reactively I slapped him across the face. I couldn't believe it! After everything I had done for him…

We sat in silence for a long time, continuing our procession past rolling farms and majestic, timeworn farmhouses where undoubtedly the farmer's daughter and the traveling salesman were fulfilling the prophecy as foretold by Henny Youngman. At least that's what I thought was out there. It was very dark and I actually couldn't see a thing.

After about an hour, I felt like my point had been made. "We cool now?" I asked him.

He just stared straight ahead, but I understood.

We were heading south but I was starting to wonder if we were *getting* anywhere. Perhaps I had made a mistake. In about two hours we would be at the state line and that's where I planned to end this quixotic journey. The duck had turned out to be a terrible travel partner. Whenever I tried to sing along with Kenny, the duck jumped right in and took the high parts, even when I'd already called them. He had no right to the radio either; he'd contributed nothing for gas so far. Plus, he had this arrogance about him that made one understand why he was on that street corner alone.

Even with all of that, I still felt a little guilty about the idea of pulling up to the state line and pushing him out the door. I decided that I would hit the next rest area so that I could gas up and buy him one last meal. Then I could make that final bit of the drive with a clear conscience while he'd have a chance to plan his next steps.

The first place we came to was not a state sanctioned rest area, just a collection of gas stations and burger joints. I pulled into the first station, but before I could open the door, the duck raised his wing, hopped out of the car, and headed inside. *Now* he decides to contribute? Was he trying to make up for the Kenny Incident or did this, perhaps, mean something more? Maybe the entire trip wasn't a fruitless exercise, maybe, just maybe, a man and a duck *could* coexist in a Ford.

I was super excited about his turn of heart and what it meant, for him, for us, for this trip, for interspecies travel partners everywhere, so I popped up out of the car to express all of this to him. As I started to yell, I realized I probably shouldn't make a big deal about things. I didn't want to embarrass him and ruin the moment. So I just shouted, "Hey, grab me a Slim Jim. Please?"

I waited for some acknowledgement, but wasn't surprised at not receiving any as the duck continued his march inside under the cover of a trucker's pregnant man-stomach. The euphoria I initially felt drained away. I expected too much, I always did. I *should* have been happy that he was finally participating, but the aloofness with which he did it frustrated me. Somewhere along the drive I had created in my head a grand quest, some Arthurian adventure, but here I was, at the end just looking for a moral victory by hoping a duck would bring me a Slim Jim.

The screams were what I heard first, followed by the piercing wails of an alarm. Looking toward the station, I registered the duck, run-waddling toward the car, quacking wildly, and carrying two bags. My instincts took over. I jumped into the car and sped into the duck's path. People were flowing out the door, including one man who appeared to be bleeding heavily, and they all seemed focused on the duck.

I tried to rectify what was taking place:

1. The duck was famous (Television? Model in ads for sporting goods stores?), and he had been recognized.
2. We happened into a weird sort of street theatre.
3. This was the beginning of the formation of an angry mob.

Based on the amount of yelling, and the appearance in the crowd of mops, brooms, and other cleaning supplies being brandished as weapons, I was leaning toward option three. Using all of the skills I learned watching *Knight Rider*, I spun the car around the last bank of gas pumps, and in the same motion, threw the passenger door open. The duck fluttered in and I hit the gas. We were doing about a thousand out of the parking lot and off toward the freeway.

As the surroundings blurred past we started laughing uncontrollably. I had no idea what had happened but it was an exhilarating feeling. When we were confident no one was behind us, we slowed down so as not to attract any new attention to ourselves. The duck reached into a bag and produced a Slim Jim. He *had* heard. There was no time to process this though, as the duck then did the most remarkable thing—he turned the bags upside down and money came fluttering down on the seat. The front seat was awash in green. I kept picking it up and setting it down, unsure if it was real or not. The duck watched proudly, throwing his head back and letting loose a deep, guttural laugh as he grabbed a wingful of money and threw it in the air. He looked at me and smiled a broad, and under any other circumstance disturbing, smile.

I wasn't myself. Some primal instinct had taken over. I no longer felt like I was just aimlessly driving a duck around, I felt a direction in life, a purpose. I felt alive. We needed more.

We pulled up to a combination gas station, 24-hour restaurant, car/truck wash, souvenir shop, trucker shower, and live bait store. The duck wasn't inside more than three minutes. I was starting to believe that he'd done this before. Just like that, we were back on the highway and a whole lot richer.

"You are amazing," I told him. "How do you even do this, considering you're, well, you know…" As the words left my mouth, I realized the awkwardness of the question. Graciously, he let it drop.

I talked excitedly about what I might buy with my share. Before we knew it, an hour had passed but more importantly, we were just a couple of miles away from another exit. There was the standard assortment of businesses, nothing special about them, but I just had a sudden, bad feeling.

"I don't think we should press our luck," I stated. "We've done pretty well so far."

The duck looked at me pleadingly. How could I resist?

A few minutes later, we were off the highway and pulling into the gas station. The duck didn't even bother to wait for the car to stop before jumping out. He waddled purposefully inside. Our success had given him a confidence, it made him emboldened. It also made him sloppy. Gunshots rang out.

I revved the engine as the duck came stumbling wildly out of the building. He jumped in and I floored it. Something smacked into the back of the car but I didn't dare slow down or look back. The duck was on the floor of the passenger side, curled into a ball, breathing heavily. His whole body shook.

"What is wrong with you?!" I screamed. I was dripping sweat, my hands were shaking, my heart pounding, but I couldn't stop. We needed to put some distance between us and whatever had happened back there.

The duck looked regretful, shameful. We drove in silence. He reached under his left wing and produced a Slim Jim. How could I be mad?

I helped him onto the seat and then found one of those radio shows you only find by accident in the middle of the night. People called in with items they were looking to buy, or sell, or trade. The simplicity of the whole affair had a calming effect.

We drove until our eyes were heavy. I found one of those forgotten exits: a few quiet houses, large open fields. We took cover under a patch of willows, and through the branches you could watch the night sky wake from its dreamtime.

I looked over at the duck. He was already asleep. He looked so peaceful. And delicious.

ROAD CREW

Brad Pauquette

Eight men sit on straw bales and upturned wooden crates on the back of the flatbed truck. Seven pairs of anxious eyes watch Jason, who takes a drag from the cigarette that hangs precariously from the corner of his mouth. His ragged red hair hangs long in the back, with the bangs in the front haphazardly chopped short to keep the hair out of his face. His eyes glisten black in the light from the moon.

The old Chevy 6500 had once been a flatbed tow truck. Ten years earlier it would have sat on the side of the road hauling up a broken down passenger sedan. Now it sits on the side of the road with a bed full of tattered and broken men, their seats encircling a crate that sits on the steel deck.

Strapped to the cab are four 55-gallon drums of diesel fuel, only one of them empty. The men never have any trouble finding diesel fuel when they need it, as they amble along the deserted roadways, headed toward nowhere, searching to stay alive. It isn't diesel they need, it isn't tools, or boots, or bullets or even cigarettes. They always find plenty of those things.

Something else accounts for the solemn candor of Jason's voice.

He looks each man in the eyes through the cloud of smoke from his cigarette, and gives the same practiced speech he always does.

"In my hand are a group of straws, one of which is shorter than the others," he tells them flatly. "We're hungry, now more than ever, and we will not starve as a group to save one man. And we will not allow ourselves to devolve into chaos and anarchy. Our team is the only advantage we have against everything out here. We all agree on this."

All of the heads around the circle nod as Jason once more looks from face to face. The last face he looks into belongs to his brother Michael, who sits to his right. Normally, Jason makes no special distinction for his brother, but on this night, he hesitates, gaze fixed on his brother's dark eyes.

Michael still has the curly blond hair of a boy, which he keeps cut short as best he can, though his beard is filling in red like his brother's and he's long been a man. Michael nods his agreement to his brother, who holds his gaze a beat longer and nods back.

Three weeks ago had been a blessing. God had dropped a meal into their lap.

Jason and Michael sprinted down the road toward the gunshot. When they finally stopped by the body and recovered their breath, Jason said, "That's a freebie."

It was Nathan. He'd been shot with his dick hanging out of his jeans, taking a piss into the ditch. It was his own fault for walking that far from the truck just to relieve himself. Everyone else knew to stay close to the truck, hell, stay on the truck if you can help it, but Nathan always had to walk a hundred yards down the road.

"That tiny wiener finally caught up with him," Michael laughed and said through a hacking cough. "If he'd had a regular size dick, he wouldn't have had to walk so far—" Michael stopped short and his head jerked up. He pointed down the road, where a man held a young boy and ran as fast as he could, dodging off the road and into the trees a quarter mile down the way. Michael wiped the dribble from his chin brought forth by the coughing fit. "Should we get him?" he asked, reaching for the pistol at his side and hunkering down to run.

Jason reached out and put his arm across Michael's chest. Michael raised up and Jason hesitated.

"We got a meal, let's leave it at that." Jason had killed many men, most without hesitation, and a few boys as well. He looked around to make sure that he and Michael were still alone. "I'd take no pleasure in dealing with that boy," he said. Michael nodded and bent down to grasp Nathan's body under the arms.

"Nathan was a dick," Michael told his brother, "can't say I'm sorry to see he's dead, and I certainly ain't sorry for such a clean wound through the middle of his forehead."

"It's a freebie, alright," Jason said. "Can't say it wasn't likely he'd be pulling the short straw tonight had this not happened. At least he got to go this way..." They dragged the body through the gray ash that covered the road, back to the truck.

Sitting on the flatbed in the commingling light of the moon, Jason places a snub-nose .38 revolver on the crate in the middle of the group and continues his speech.

"We will each draw a straw and keep it concealed in one hand. When I am holding the last straw, we will all reveal our straws at the same time. Whichever man is holding the smallest straw will stand courageously, while the rest begin counting to ten as a group. If the chosen man wishes, he may pick up this pistol, put it to his own head and leave us on his own terms. However, when the group reaches ten, if he has not picked up the pistol and provided for us, the man to his right must pick up the pistol on his behalf, place it to the chosen one's head, and pull the trigger."

Most of the men had heard this speech eleven times before, though some had been added to the crew more recently. Nonetheless, each man reacted—fidgeting, spitting or wiping compulsively at his nose—each one fidgeting in his own way.

"We all agree on this?" Jason asked, once again looking from face to face, into glassy eyes—each one nodding in affirmation.

Three weeks ago Jason and Michael had dragged Nathan's body back to the truck, and the rest of the crew had prepared the body for Michael's task.

Nathan was once a big man. As Michael poked his knife into the cooling body, he noticed how the skin bunched around the wrists.

The head and the hands had already been removed by two other men and buried in the woods. Without them, it was just a slab of meat hanging by a rope from a tree, by the time the skin was removed it could pass for any animal. Michael completed the skin-deep slit from the wrist up to the armpit, and began peeling away the skin, revealing lean, stringy muscles clinging to the bones. Michael pulled at the arm muscles, probing their density and shook his head.

This task always fell to Michael. He said he didn't mind it, and it gave him an excuse to avoid the duties that he liked even less. "I'll butcher the dead men, y'all can butcher the live ones," he once told his brother two hours after they'd found an old bottle of Ezra Brooks whiskey in the pantry of an abandoned house.

Michael completed the job quickly and with practice. He set aside a good portion of the thighs for a roast that night, packed the ribs in salt to be used in a day or two, and the rest he carefully shaved into thin strips to be dried into jerky.

A grown man, thinned by starvation and cannibalism, only yields about sixty pounds of edible meat. Divided between eight men, with little else for sustenance, the meat Michael peeled from Nathan's emaciated body lasted no more than ten days.

When each man was left with a small pouch of stringy jerky, they had found another body along the road, this one lying on its back under a bridge. Years ago, the overpass would have been crowded with cars and trucks hurrying to and from whatever desolated American city sat in the distance. But as they approached the body, the only sound in the world was the pip-pop of the old diesel engine. When Jason killed the engine, the sound dissipated into the spoliated landscape, as if absorbed by the barren trees and shrubs that lined the road.

Michael was the first out of the back of the truck, pistol drawn as he approached the makeshift tent beside the rotting body. He smelled the air as if for predators, and recoiled, using one hand to pull the handkerchief up from his neck to cover his face.

Jason pulled up his handkerchief and unholstered his sidearm, shortly behind Michael, while the rest of the men spread out to form a loose perimeter around the entrance to the underpass, as if by instinct. The men looked on as Jason and Michael stepped under the bridge.

"Lucky bastard," Jason told his brother as they stood over the body.

Michael laughed. "Poor bastard, I'd say," he said as he poked at the body with his foot. The skin on the face of the man before them was gaunt and white, with an unnatural green hue below the eyes, which were permanently open—their gaze affixed to a water pipe dripping sewage thirty feet away. Michael pulled out his knife and probed the skin around the man's neck, the blade slipping easily in and splitting the skin like paper. "He ain't no good to us, that's for damn sure."

Jason kicked over the tent to reveal a dozen cans of food, neatly stacked. "Ain't much left out here." He looked around the space with practiced efficiency, confirming that there was no danger, and motioned for the rest of the crew to come forward.

The men ambled toward the body and began to sort through the rest of the man's goods, though there wasn't much they could use. They had plenty of clothes, but they picked through them nonetheless. Spare matches, a badly rusted pocket knife, half of an unbreakable hair comb.

Jason stood back as they cataloged and sorted each item. He noted how each man looked at the stack of cans and then subconsciously fingered the pouch of jerky bulging in his pocket.

"Few more days at least," one of them muttered.

"Thank God for a few more days," Michael said, then he looked back toward his brother. "It's been a whole lot of a few more days, and we're still not lying on the side of the road like this poor bastard. Ain't that right, Jason? Alone, each one of us would have been just like this fucker, getting picked through on the side of the road. At least together we got a few more days. Never know what tomorrow might bring, just so's you're alive to see it."

Jason nodded to his brother, turned and walked back to the truck.

Before the meeting was called, and the men assembled on the truck, Jason and Michael walked down the road by themselves. It had been three days since any man had eaten anything, everyone knew what was coming.

A quarter mile down the road, Jason veered off the road and into the woods with his brother. "What's going on?" Michael asked. Jason looked at him and shook his head, they continued on through the woods.

Finally, Jason stopped in a little clearing with several fallen logs. They sat down and Michael took a long pull from his water bottle.

"You know why they trust us?" Jason asked after his brother recapped his bottle.

Michael shrugged. "We're the best. They need us."

Jason shook his head. "They trust us because we take the most risk. They trust us because when there's something to be done, we're the first ones to start and the last ones to stop. They trust us because we earn it."

Michael pawed at his nose, smearing sweat across his face.

"Why do you take the first straw?" Jason asked him.

Michael shrugged again. "Because a long time ago you told me to. You told me to set a good example. I take the first one, you take the last one."

"That's right. It's where our power comes from. We always carry the heaviest load. We earn it every time we're the first ones through the door of a vacant house, or the last ones to fill our canteens." Jason paused and chose his words. "How come one of us has never pulled the short straw?"

Once again, Michael shrugged. "Because I always take the one you tell me to." Michael laughed. "You gonna tell me?"

Jason nodded. "Yeah, little brother. I'm gonna tell you." He pulled a handful of dark brown plastic straws from his pocket, the kind that years ago would have been used for stirring coffee. "The odds of pulling the straw are the lowest with the first straw. That's why you pull it. It makes you look brave, and you're unlikely to pull it." Jason laid the straws out one by one in his hand, and then bunched them up into a tight clump. "I always come to the meeting with the straws in my hand. You know where to pull from, last time I told you to pull a straw that's close to me, so I made sure to lay them out beforehand so that the straw wouldn't be in that section." Jason closed his hand around the straws. "I know where the short straw is."

"Yeah, but what about you? How come you never get left with the short straw? You don't get to pick."

Now it was Jason's turn to shrug. "When a bunch of guys all have to draw something at the same time, most of the time they'll all grab the one closest to them, or at least one on their side. Every once in a while somebody will reach across to pull one, but my odds are as good as yours. Mostly I just get lucky."

Michael smiled at his brother. "How'd you figure that out?"

"I guess I just got lucky the first few times," Jason hung his head and massaged his coarse red hair. "I guess I still been..."

Jason pulled a pack of cigarettes from his pocket and shook one out. He offered one to Michael, who declined. "Make my head spin when we ain't eaten like this."

They sat in silence while Jason smoked. Finally Michael asked, "Who's it gonna be tonight?"

Jason looked at his brother distantly, as though at a spirit drawn up by a medium.

"Rob's been bitchin' a lot," Michael blurted. "Frankly, don't know that he'd mind that much."

Jason nodded, his eyes rheumy and distant. "Just take one from your side tonight."

On the flatbed in the moonlight, Jason stubs out his cigarette with his right hand. His left holds the straws. He grabs the pack of cigarettes from his inside pocket, flicks one out with his thumb and grabs it from the pack with his lips. While everyone watches nervously, he puts the pack back in his pocket, produces a lighter and lights the cigarette.

"Well let's get on with it then," one of the men says.

"Got somewhere else to be?" Jason asks. The men chuckle nervously.

Jason holds his left hand up, with eight plastic drinking straws sticking out. On his own initiative, Michael stands bravely, snags the closest straw from Jason's hand and sits back down. His eyes shift from man to man as he watches the scene unfold. The corner of his mouth twitches only slightly as each man takes the straw closest to him and conceals it in his hand. His eyes tick nervously to his brother's face, but Jason stares only at the remaining straw protruding from his clenched fist.

Jason closes his thumb over the remaining straw, his fingernail crusted with grime. No one moves a muscle, instead all the men stare misty-eyed at Jason's face, gaze fixed somewhere below his eyes, waiting for him to nod, for the judgment to be made.

When Jason speaks, the men grimace. "This is the last ten seconds of one of our lives. It's been an honor surviving with you, I pray that the sacrifice will not be made in vain." With that he nods, and the men look into their hands.

At once, a sigh of relief escapes the group as each man looks into his own hand. Eyes dart around the circle, seeking out the shortened straw, then flash from rapture to confusion to anger when they can't find it. Finally, all eyes land on Jason's clenched fist, still concealing the straw within.

Jason nods his head and pulls his cigarette to his mouth. He takes a long drag, then plucks it from his mouth and stubs it out deliberately on the bed of the truck. He runs his hand through his coarse red hair, just like he's done a thousand times.

Michael's bottom lip is between his teeth, the skin dimpled and red where his incisors dig in. He lifts his hand to his face as one of the men in the group says *one*.

Michael's eyes dart around the group as the other men join in chorus *two*. Jason sits stoic and still as the men continue to count, but Michael clenches his teeth, the air escaping in hastened breaths, clutching his short blond hair in his hands above his forehead.

The men continued to count, growing in volume with each digit.

"No," Michael whispers at first. "No," he turns and says to all of them. "No!" he yells. He drops to a knee in front of his seat and lunges for the pistol positioned on the crate in front of him. But quick as lightning, Jason snatches the gun. He rises to his feet while his brother drops to his knees. Michael pleads with his eyes, a solitary tear welling up in his left eye.

"Later on, little brother," Jason says. As the men count *eight*, it is as if the sound of the men and the night fade away. Jason whispers to his brother, "Earn it."

A shot rings out through the night, and Jason's body slumps to the old tow truck's deck. A silence falls over the men as the blood congeals on the stainless steel, and they wait with heads bowed.

Michael lies silently with his face pressed to the cold metal bed of the old Chevy. The men wait as the silence of the night resumes around them.

One of the men rises and moves toward Jason's body. He nods his head to two others for help. The men hoist Jason's body down from the truck and begin to carry it toward the woods. Before they reach the treeline, Michael rises. He plucks a nylon rope from the deck, tosses it to one of the men and points to a large oak twenty yards in.

"That one. Not too high," he says.

The man who caught the rope nods his head, and walks into the woods with the body.

Michael climbs down from the bed and pulls the case containing his butchering knives from behind the seat of the truck. He pulls his handkerchief up over his face and walks toward the woods, the moonlight glistening off of his brown eyes.

CRACKED BLACKTOP

Ed Davis

The bus ride is excruciating. The band plays poker endlessly and consumes cases and cases of beer—but no cigarettes. Signs are everywhere in Dad's cryptic hand: "Here lies the hide of the last SOB who smoked on this bus." I gaze beyond the rain-webbed glass, hunker lower in my seat behind the driver. I try writing—the idea of doing some journalism hits me (an ecclesiastical *Electric Kool-Aid Acid Test*?)—then reading, but so far the Bible on the seat beside me—the Thompson chain-reference red-letter edition that Mim got me our first Christmas as a married couple—remains unopened. Finally I settle for gawking at rain-ruined cornfields and leafless trees on Route 52 along the Ohio River. At least it isn't snowing. A blizzard before Christmas is all we need.

Dad keeps to his little closet of a room in back, ostensibly writing. But there hasn't been an album of new material in six or seven years, just rehashed compilations, an album of traditional tunes from the British Isles and Greatest Hits, Volumes Ten and Eleven. I try to fathom what it must be like to live decades beyond mega-popularity, to stand up and sing those ancient chestnuts to graying masses of people who come not to experience cutting-edge art, but to gawk at a legend and be reassured that, if Israel Jones still lives and breathes (more or less), they might be immortal, too. I'm a bit jealous, I admit. You have to be an *is* before you can become a *been*, and I was and am neither. I'm the "son of"—a great liability in the music biz.

Tracing the golden letters of my name on the book beside me, I'm thinking of Dad's old black Bible with pale drink rings on its cover when a voice interrupts.

"Hey, Reverend, mind if I set down?"

Startled out of my reverie, I stare up slack-jawed into the face of the wavy-blond-haired rhythm guitarist.

"Please do."

"Shit, I'm sorry," he says, reaching down to hand me the Thompson. "Oh, damn, pardon my French." He puts his hand over his mouth like a kid caught cussing in church.

"Don't sweat it. I'm not that kind of reverend." *What kind are you?* I wonder, not for the first time, *one who doesn't believe in hell or the devil, who isn't totally sure there's an afterlife and who hasn't been able to pray—* not really—*in months.* Recently I've found myself returning to my nihilistic pre-seminary undergrad days as a philosophy major and self-styled cynic: over-educated and spiritually dead.

He sits gingerly, as if my Bible were still there, and his butt might wrinkle Genesis. "What basically are you, then?" Sweet sincerity ripples in waves around him. I remember what it was like being on this bus when I was seventeen—tough as a nut outside, all mama's boy mush within—but mostly just stoned.

"I guess I accept the world on the world's terms," I say.

He looks puzzled. "Is that Catholic?"

"AA."

He glances away, out the opposite window. I don't blame him. Before I found the fellowship, the last thing in the world I wanted was somebody preaching that crap.

He lifts his beer to his lips. "You mind?"

"It's a long way to Cincinnati."

"We've never played there. I mean, *I've* never played there. I've only been with Boss for a year."

"A great equal-opportunity employer, isn't he?" I say before I think better of it. "Union-scale pay, health insurance, disability, retirement with stock options." His look of bewilderment almost softens me.

"Actually, Reverend, he's paying me cash. See, I'm sort of on probation, on account, mostly, of the last guitar player who Boss had to fire. Nathan would, like, come late to gigs and stuff." Blondie shakes his head as if he's described a heretic. "You just can't believe anybody'd do that, would you, working for, you know, somebody like your old man?"

"Beyond belief." Irony is probably a language as lost on the kid as Urdu. He's part of Dad's endlessly self-renewing fountain of youth: pluck kids loaded with talent from their mama's breast to come make you sound/look young again. Let them do all the heavy lifting while you prowl the stage looking legendary. And howl. But I find myself warming to the boy, against my better judgment. (Maybe he'll come in handy, I think, the angel on my shoulder shaking his head at my cynicism.)

"I'm Thom," I say, offering him a hand.

"Patrick." He offers me five damp fingers.

"By the way," he says, "nice suit."

"Thank you."

"But why're you wearing it now, since this ain't exactly a church?"

I mime astonishment. "You don't think it's right for a rock tour?"

The kid actually blushes. "Well, I mean, you know…"

"I'm kidding, Pat. I'm used to being treated as different. I walk into a sickroom or a wake and the conversation stops. *He's* here. Time to get holy."

"I'm sorry, Rev."

"I like it sometimes. Makes me different." From *him,* I don't say. "But you guys," I wave my hand to include everyone, "don't make me feel different, because you're still doing what you did before I got here."

"That's for damn—darn—sure." He casts a glance over his shoulder, but the only sound now is the slow slap of cards.

"So what's it like, this gig?" I ask genially, now that we've bonded.

"Oh, man, I love playing with someone you never know what they're gonna do. I mean, your dad never does a song the same way twice. It could even be in a different key, with a totally new rhythm, new chords, verses where choruses used to be and—"

"Screeches and moans for lyrics."

He nods. "Boss can be a tad bit weird at times, but he's still original as all get-out. He's a force of the universe."

I take the deepest breath I can get, which isn't deep enough, because my mind careens into a tirade. *So you don't mind playing behind a has-been rock star whose heart could explode at any moment; who's jerked his loyal fans around throughout his career by baiting them with lyrics that could mean this, could mean that, in the end probably don't mean anything; the same legend who's berated his audiences to get a life, think for themselves or blow their brains out at concerts where the front row paid a hundred and fifty bucks a head; a man who walked out on his fragile wife and five-year-old son in order to live free as the wind and sow his seed across five continents, leaving at least a score of children and bereft mothers without alimony in his wake?*

I've had too much caffeine; my hands are shaking. I haven't surrendered to self-pity like this since I told Dad off at a rest stop outside Albuquerque over two decades ago, when I quit the Eternal Tour forever (or so I'd thought). As I sink back into the Naugahyde cushion, I regret including the lovely wife—my doomed mom—in my tirade. I'm glad I didn't berate this boy beside me, who only did what I'd done at his age: fallen in love with the world's most seductive quasi-religion.

"Look," I say, reaching out to squeeze his arm, "I have a few issues with my father. Dad's not God."

His eyebrows lift. "I'll say. He can be pretty naughty."

I almost fall off my seat. "*Naughty?*"

"I mean, I really like the way he's working these wacko kids who show up to cut themselves while we play. Heck, maybe they'll even git neckid tonight."

I was hardly ready for young people slashing their faces with razorblades last night at Charleston's Coal Palace while Dad howled. Praise the Lord I hadn't been close enough to see, not really. *Exciting them to violence,* the voice on the phone had said. I look back out the window. We are apparently still on the outskirts of hell, the huge cones of a nuke plant passing us beside blasted burnt fields some farmer recently torched.

"Your daddy teach you to play?" Patrick asks.

"How did you know?"

"Oh, *man*," he punches my arm hard. "I got Subterfuge's album. Great sh—stuff. Bet you learned everything you needed to know right at the foot of the master."

I can't tell him the truth—not in the face of that wide-open, innocent grin of his.

"He was a mighty tough task-master, Patrick."

His eyes glaze. *Oh, please, please,* they say, *toss me some nugget from the treasure-trove of His Legendariness.*

"I can tell," he says, "from your CD!"

I cringe. After the drubbing it took from the pens of the critics, comparing me to HIM mercilessly, I trashed every copy I'd owned. "Well, I tried to play a little harmonica..."

"Tried! On 'Wounded Knees' you sounded better'n Delbert McClinton. And you bent notes better'n Howlin' Wolf on 'Trial and Terror.' A lot better'n you played guitar." He hangs his head for a second. "Sorry, man. I mean, in my opinion."

"It's all right. The almighty arbiters of taste at *Rolling Stone* totally agree with you. But my father didn't."

"'Course not. He seen you as a rival. Y'know, the son trying to knock off the old man. He prob'ly didn't take lightly to that."

This time I hardly feel Patrick's shy fist strike my sleeve. "Man, you were hard-headed to keep on going after that."

He looks so earnest it banishes my anger and shame. For an instant, I hear myself drawing and blowing like the bellows of hell at the back of the bus on the corroded old Hohner I'd found beneath a seat, squeezing, bending, uselessly striving to make music out of air and failing so miserably that *somebody* had to intervene. Somebody like my Dad.

"Anyhow, that's how I come to hear your CD—mandatory listening." He giggles. "Swear to God, that's what Boss said, 'Mandatory,' you know, in the voice of God. Like those NFL guys have to watch all that film of other teams, we have to listen to your CD." He laughs full-tilt this time. "Glad you only made one!"

I feel light-headed. Dad *liked* my playing! Unbelievable. The boy beside me waxes silent for several seconds. "Maybe *you're* why he quit playing the harp."

"Yeah, right."

"You don't think your dad's proud of you, man? All right, then explain something."

And before I could implore him not to do whatever shameful act he was about to commit, he was gone. Within a few card-slaps he was back, laying a huge photograph album on top of my Bible. He flops down, grinning.

"Discovered this one day in the middle of a stack of *Playboys* when I was bored outta my frickin' mind. G'wan. See what your dad thought about you."

In a memory sharp as a Polaroid, I see Mom, twin braids flopping beside her face, urging me to open presents. Birthday, Christmas, she always loved to watch me. But where was Dad when that happened? He's not in the picture at all. I take a big breath and open the album. The first photo, black and white, shows me holding the black Stratocaster I got on my tenth birthday. Mom laughs in the background; she said she'd made him wait a decade to give me such a gift, to make sure it was right. My first electric guitar (I'd had a half-sized acoustic since I was old enough to walk). In the picture, I am watching my short, thick fingers fret. Memory jabs me again: I recall Dad behind the camera, and he is smiling.

"Guess that's you as Clapton, Rev."

Patrick's chuckle brings me back. And though I've seen enough, I dutifully thumb through the book, marveling where and how Dad obtained a particular shot—me in the talent show, at my first band's first paid gig, rehearsing with Subterfuge in the studio, on tour at small clubs, me singing, wailing on the harp, smoking, drinking whiskey, grinning goofily, never sober after that first birthday photo. Where'd Dad get all these? He was never there. My late mother surely found, saved, clipped and sent them all to him. He probably had one of his backup singers assemble the whole shebang for him. At last I close the book with relief, knowing I'll never open it again, knowing it's drawn blood. Before I think better of it, I speak.

"The first time he heard me play harp, he screamed at me. The second time he slapped me so hard my ears rang. And the third time, he ripped it out of my mouth—nearly took out an incisor—and threw it out the bus window."

The bus explodes with laughter. I glance up to see the driver in the rearview lower his guilty eyes and tighten his quivering mouth. They've been listening! Of course. They probably couldn't wait to see my reaction to Boss's ode to nostalgia they've had flung in their faces forever. *Philistines.* Shame flashes. It quickly turns to anger, then rage. I'd been the one to find my mother in the bathtub that day, more blood than water. Too late to save her, of course—he'd killed her a decade earlier when he'd left for good. *Yes, I had a few issues.*

As my eyes blur, I return to the first page. I need to see the three of us sitting around that oak table where Mom would soon serve up chocolate cake with white icing, my favorite. Dad would pick up a book, and I'd pretend to be lead picking. (He didn't buy me an amp for another six months—"Why hear bad *loud*?" he said behind his newspaper.)

"Maybe you should set in with us sometime, Reverend."

His grin might be sincere or might be a smirk. Humbled by the band's laughter, I'm not inclined to ask. I let my hand drift up to my chest where the harp lies in my shirt pocket, warm as a pistol, behind the cigarette-pack-sized, leather-bound Book of Psalms above my heart.

"Well, nice talking to you, Rev. I'd better put this back in the stack or your old man might kill me."

He removes the binder, uncovering my Bible, the white pages with so much black type a counter-point to the images I've just seen. The words blur, become notes, and I feel like sleeping for a very long time.

28

§

Last night at the Coal Palace, it was easier for me to hide. McGillicuddy's stage doesn't really have wings, so Murphy, Dad's manager, gets me a stool at the rear in the corner. In the darkness, out of the spots, I'll look like a guitar tech.

"Getcha some soda water or somethin' before I get the hell out of here?" Murphy asks.

I give him my most ministerially disapproving stare. "You're not staying?"

He keeps his gaze level. "Legend ain't good enough. Gotta be God now. I ain't watchin' it."

"Dad said that he's God?"

Murphy shrugs. "Not exactly. Said something like it was God speaking through him when he does that howlin' thing."

"My father, as you know, has never been one to avoid the outrageous, especially if media are lurking."

"Huh-uh. He told me this one night before beddy-bye, all seriousness just before he zonked out."

"So he never actually said he's God, but that God speaks through him?"

"Same difference. Still loony."

§

If the congregation of Holy Martyrs could only see their slightly graying pastor, poised on the threshold of forty, cowering against the back wall at an Israel Jones concert, my *father's* concert. They think my father is dead, and, until I received that call, he was. I'd finished preaching Wednesday night prayer meeting and returned to the office to find my friend Deacon Henry Owens counting the offering, when the phone rang.

"Holy Martyrs, this is Reverend Thomas Johnson," I said, watching Henry's broad back at the table across from my desk. I heard nothing, or, rather, the nothing that is tense waiting. But all the tension was on the other end—I was calm, even relaxed. My sermon on Jonah's pride had gone well.

"May I help you?" I said. The same silence, as if something coiled, waiting to spring. I tried again. "How may I be of service to you?"

"Your father." Female, throaty and low.

"Are you a doctor?" I asked.

"You'd better go to him. He's going off the deep end."

I laughed bitterly and watched Henry sit up straighter. "He lives on the deep end. Has there been another incident?" That's what they'd called the first heart attack, before they'd known: a cardiac incident.

My caller seemed to ponder. Henry had resumed counting.

"He's exciting them to violence."

I let that hang in the charged air for a second before answering. "Last I heard he's on tour, doing fine." Any time I got on the Internet, I always checked out his tour schedule.

"You'd better go to him." A breathy whisper. Was she crying?

I'd leaned back in my desk chair. "May I ask to whom I'm speaking?" Watching his back, I was certain now Henry was waiting, too.

"A friend."

That was all. When I hung up, Henry resumed counting. Keeping my eyes averted from the deacon's back, I reached inside my desk and found my father's last birthday card: geese on a lake. The cards had started coming in '01—the year of his first heart attack, the last time I'd seen him—and had come right on time every year since, signed "Dad" with a P.S.: Murphy's cellphone number. I waited until Henry was gone before punching in the numbers I thought I'd never use.

"Skipper—I mean Reverend—your daddy's acting mighty weird."

I snorted into the phone, not just because he'd used the nickname I hadn't heard in a couple of decades. "Murphy, my father left weird in the lurch around 1973."

"This is different. You gotta see it to believe it."

See my dad after five years of silence? The palm of my hand gripping the receiver was sweating. "Is he doing anything that would incite violence?"

"No more'n usual."

"Where is he?"

"Charleston, West Virginia. He was s'posed to play the Civic Center, but crowds have thinned lately, and it was moved to the Carson Coal Palace."

I closed my eyes. A dump. In the fifties, it had been the site of grand culture in the heart of the Appalachian coalfields, but when I played there with Subterfuge in the seventies, it already smelled of mildew, the seats torn, their stuffing coming out.

I had hospital visits, prayer meeting…but I had no family to tell goodbye, and I could always get some retired pastor to sub for me. (It would also be good to get out of Dodge and forget my own troubles for a while.) Plus, I wanted to ask my father what I'd never had the guts to: *Dad, why'd you kill Mom by abandoning her when she needed you most?* Incredible as it still sounds to me now, I wanted an apology, *needed* it like a junkie needs the next needle.

"When's the gig?" I asked.

"Friday night, eight o'clock."

I knew if I started asking questions, I'd never go. Murphy spoke before I could.

"Meet me at seven-thirty sharp at the back door. Look for the bus."

"It's December, Murph. Don't leave me out there waiting."

"We'll be watching for you."

"All right."

The hand that hung up was shaking.

§

I can no longer hear my own thoughts. All I can hear are shouts of *Is-reel* above the banging of beer bottles on tabletops and stomping feet, the noise rocking my bones. I am comforted that Murphy isn't too far away, maybe outside in the alley, listening through a headset, or somewhere above us in the light booth or hovering over the sound man, suggesting a bit more monitor so Boss can hear how bad he sounds and shape the hell up. Brutus won't stray too far from his Caesar.

The poor kid who's the opening act can't do anything to suit the mob. They're about a chorus away from stoning him when he finally shambles off. I wonder if the cutters have gotten in—a perfect venue for them, since they can get up close and personal, but also one where the consequences of their antics could be more costly. At a private club, they can be bounced onto their bleeding ears rather than escorted out the door. On the other hand, they might be tolerated, even enjoyed (I shudder). I'm not going to be ambushed tonight—I am ready.

Or I think I am. For several seconds, I find myself itching to ease off my stool, unpocket my harp, palm that bullet and squawl, smash bricks and mortar to bits with spears of sound, glittering riffs, howling growls. My palms are sweating, my throat constricts and I am right back on the road, right where I'd left off at the bitter end of the eighties. Shaking my head violently to clear it of demons, I return in time to see the band walk onstage.

As before, Dad comes last, and the place goes nuts when, after strapping on his Gibson, he lifts his right hand in silent consecration.

I confess my pride. I scream inside, *You'd better love this man who's given you not just his nervous system but HIS SOUL. You'd better appreciate it.* But they don't. They can't. Imprisoned in vanity and sin, they project their needs onto their hero to save themselves. But a hero—and my Dad isn't one—can't save you; only Christ can. Oh, I can be righteous when I get going. And I am in tip-top Moses-on-the-mountain mode. Before "Dead Man's Blues" is twelve bars down the road, the Bleeding Boy and Girl Scouts materialize from their corner and stand shimmying before the stage, only a foot or so above the floor. Reflexively, I pat my pocketful of Psalms right next to the harp. I've foresworn my need to ignite a crowd—but my father? He must know he's the flame beneath tinder. I want these infidels gone, these last gasps of Sodom and Gomorrah.

Dad is singing now, actually enunciating. And the young ones—vampirish in their chopped, spiky green and purple and blond hair, nose-rings and tattoos, vapors and veils—prance and sway, the spotlights illuminating faces agog with ecstasy. Is my father, in truth, inspired by them? Does he even *see* them?

The song ends, and the place erupts like gunfire. I find myself wishing it *were* gunfire, scourging this iniquitous den, myself included, myself especially. I've whipped myself into a frenzy of guilty self-loathing for not telling the legend exactly what I think. *You could stop this now*, I should've told him back there on the bus, *before somebody gets hurt.* I can only pray I'll have another chance.

From the next song, "Stripped, Whipped and Hungover in the Waco County Jail," I know, this set, he will take no prisoners. He blazes through one rocker after another, even covering the Stones' "Hang Fire" and Neil Young's "Like a Hurricane," driving the audience into a frenzy.

At last Dad seems to be winding down, as he launches into a lush, lovely arrangement of "The Garden," ostensibly about a fighter in Madison Square Garden, but suggesting Gethsemane with the lines, "I prayed, let me go/even though the willing sacrifice must believe what he cannot see." After the seventh verse, he steps away from the mic to become the diminutive boy-folksinger he'd been four decades ago, just a voice, a guitar and tongue afire. When he unstraps the Gibson, the crowd, thinking the show over, begins to stomp and scream. His back stiffens as his head rolls back on his shoulders, his graying blond mane alabaster in the white spot. His legs pump and his heels click on the wood as he does some sort of jittery jig.

The bleeders—I've dubbed them the Furies—now stand at the edge of the low stage, swaying before him. A beautiful latte-colored girl stands a mere twelve or so feet away from my father, her hand outstretched, reaching slim, trembling fingers into the spotlight's glare. They curl, beckon, and importune. Then, to my amazement, the girl enters the spot's harsh glow. Dad's arm stretches toward her, where she stands, perfectly still, as small and fragile as a child. His fingers are white as bone; and though I've never seen my father implore anyone, anywhere, for any reason—his trembling fingers beckon. Time stops. No one moves, no one breathes. Stepping closer, she reaches toward him and their fingertips touch—I would laugh at such a mirroring of Michelangelo's Sistine Chapel ceiling—Adam touching God—if the scene weren't so holy and inevitable, so ready to erupt in flames. My heart skitters off-track for a couple of beats; then, finding its rhythm, it picks up steam, heads uphill, smoke pouring.

It's over in a second; she moves back before someone intrudes to protect the legend, for legends must be protected, always, from intimacy. But that protector isn't me. My own arm is outstretched—not to defend, I realize, but to take some of what's being offered, if there's any left. As the girl melds back into the crowd and time resumes, my arm falls limply to my side. My fingers uncurl, empty, as usual.

Then it begins. At first it seems a kind of hum beginning in Dad's nasal cavity and moving deeper into the throat where it vibrates for a time until, as his mouth opens wider, it becomes an ululation that rises and falls, like an animal with its belly slit, the sound a coyote makes after chewing off its leg in a steel trap, the scream of Jesus when the first nail struck bone.

My soul goes cold. A dull knife rakes flesh from my lower spine.

If that's all he'd done, if he'd quickly kicked off the next song, it would've been awful but bearable. Lord knows, I wanted him to get on down that cracked blacktop he'd been on all his life, all my life, just get this gig over, with as little fuss as possible. He'd been on the Eternal Tour so long—through death, divorce, debilitation, estrangement and collapse, financial and physical—that I'd decided he'd croak out here on the road, right in the middle of it, with all of *them* watching, judging, shaking their heads (how I'd hated them, especially when they'd most viciously compared me to him—what had I expected?). I'd given up years ago thinking I could save him—even after I was saved—finally deciding to let the rabble crucify him, if he didn't crucify himself first. I wondered if he wasn't perhaps begging for it now.

My eyes fill as my father utters sounds of a man having his flesh flayed. But as it continues, my scorched nerve endings cool to numbness. My arms hang limp, shorn of all strength. My legs lack the muscle to carry me outside. And as my vision clears, I focus on those standing right in front of the stage. They seem silent penitents prepared for baptism, their loose garments wavering in water.

A lanky, bald boy, at least a head taller than the others, appears to be shaving his cheek, head thrown back, golden hoops dangling from his ear, eyes closed. But as I focus more closely, I see dark trails snaking down his neck and upper chest. He is making quick incisions into his hairless face, blood running like water.

Sound goes first—then I'm gasping for air. I see a bathroom, a tubful of blood, and white, white flesh. Stars and galaxies burst at the edges of my vision, and I fear I'm going to faint. Instantly my hand covers my heart. My palm feels for and finds the as-yet-unplayed harp in my inner pocket; my fingers fondle Psalms right beside it. Thus armed, I stand, and for the moment stave off unconsciousness. In this moment, it's clear I must follow my path to Calvary to receive the thing I covet most, if not apology, then perhaps the penance alcoholics pay: living amends. I know now with the certainty that can come to the dying that I will follow my father to the end of the road.

"Cracked Blacktop" is adapted from the author's novel
The Psalms of Israel Jones
(West Virginia University Press, 2014)

JUNE

Aaron Behr

Victor passes his cane from his left to his right hand and leans his weight onto it. A sixteen wheeler speeds past him and the burst of wind knocks him a step toward the shoulder of the highway.

Bracing tight onto his cane, he takes a deep breath and continues down the long highway. It's only been a hundred feet, but every joint screams for rest.

He walks another hundred feet before he rests on his cane. The asphalt is gray, old, but not as old and gray as he. He remembers the birth of this road. That's why he is here. Not to reminisce but to see it for himself.

Highway twenty-four stretches out as far as he can see. For a Tuesday afternoon, on a four lane road, he would have expected more traffic. There are mostly semis which, aside from that last one, have been crossing into the next lane.

The highway runs down the middle of swampland. Victor turns toward it. The skeletal remains of dead trees point out of the bog. Wet, stagnant water with green moss reflects the cloud filled sky. It looks as if a film has grown over top of it.

Rotting wood and putrid water smell of sulfur—rotten eggs mixed with death. He imagines that this is how hell smells. Not of fire and brimstone, but the rotting and decay of life. He closes his eyes and remembers.

In June of 1963, Victor drove his Chevy pickup down a winding, muddy road. It was the seventh of June and already hot and humid. Both windows were rolled down and a putrid smell wafted into the cab. At first, his stomach felt weak, but over time his senses acclimated to it.

The truck rocked back and forth against the gravel. Dead leaves had spent the winter on top of that gravel. It was as if all life stopped here, that it retreated at the sight of this swamp.

Somehow, the long-dead trees provided a shade equal to that of a full oak brimming with bright green leaves. The gray that hovered over the swamp sent a fearsome chill down his spine.

He drove up a hill and slowed in front of a plain, two-story home, its whitewashed shingles spotted with hints of dark brown. Faded and functional red shutters guarded hand-blown glass windows, bulbous and distorted.

The porch was huge. It wrapped around the entire house. There was a plain blue porch swing the wind had knocked over. Gravel kicked up as he pulled up next to the front steps. In front of him, a leafless weeping willow tree towered over the house. Underneath the tree sat a baby blue 1937 Ford Coupe in perfect condition.

Victor gasped. The car, at least twenty-six years old, looked as if it had just been pulled off of a showroom floor. Absentmindedly, only focusing on the car, he opened his door. The hinges groaned in the humidity.

The gravel condensed under his footsteps. His mouth hung open as he approached the car with a reverence akin to walking into the middle of communion. He ran his fingers along the fender.

"You like her?"

The sultry voice startled Victor. He retracted his hand and looked up to the porch. A beautiful woman, with long black hair, glimmering pale skin and big beautiful blue eyes leaned on the railing of the porch. A smile filled her blush lips. Her chest pushed against the thin silk of her white slip.

Victor tried to focus on her face. He choked as he spoke, "Ma'am." He went to tip the hat that he had left in the truck in his reverie, and then it dawned on him that he had left all his important documents on the passenger seat as well.

She giggled. A wave of heat ascended Victor's back and swelled at the base of his neck. He grinned and looked down to his glossy dress shoes. He forced himself to look up at her with feigned confidence. Those merry blue eyes greeted him. "Hello ma'am, I'm Victor Crawford from the Federal Highway Administration. We sent a letter to this household about the land."

She placed her left hand on her hip and kept the other on the rail. Her expression curved to something coy. "And I didn't reply."

"So you're June Seavers?"

"I am." Her expression didn't change.

Victor shook his head and stepped closer. "I'm sorry to bother you, ma'am."

"I'm guessing you expected someone different?"

Victor nervously laughed and adjusted his tie. "I was."

"Older?"

"A bit."

She stood upright and crossed her arms. Victor was glad she did. "Well you've caught me off guard, Victor. I don't normally greet my visitors in a slip, but I don't normally have visitors."

"I'm sorry, ma'am."

"I doubt you are." She let her grin linger and her eyes scanned him. "Why don't you go get your paperwork, count to six hundred, then come to my door and knock like a proper gentleman."

Another semi screams past Victor. He rocks against his cane.

Red and blue lights follow the whoop of a siren. Victor knows he is in trouble. He's here for a purpose. But the officers will only help that purpose. He steps off the shoulder onto the soggy wet earth. There's no point walking farther. His body won't take it. To him, this place feels right.

The State Highway Patrol car slows to a stop on the shoulder a dozen feet behind him. Victor looks back and sees that it's a slick silver Mustang.

The officer climbs out of the cruiser wearing a wide-brimmed hat, a bulletproof vest bulges from his skinny body. His jawline is weak, clean shaven, with a cleft in his chin. This man hardly strikes Victor as an officer.

The officer approaches with his hands on his hips. "Afternoon."

Victor sighs.

"Are you okay?"

"I'm fine."

The officer is by Victor's side. His name badge reads, "Wheeler." Another semi speeds by and churns up the air around them. This causes a new, stronger batch of swamp fumes to engulf them. Officer Wheeler covers his nose with the back of his hand.

Victor chuckles.

"I'm Officer Wheeler."

"I read your nametag." Victor points a shaky finger at the badge.

"Good. I forget about it…" He gags a little. "That smell…"

"It's certainly pungent."

Officer Wheeler tries to shake it off. "Is that your Buick parked two hundred feet back?"

"It is."

"Did you break down?"

"No officer." Victor turns to face the man. "I had to walk out here to see it happen."

"You shouldn't be walking on the shoulder. It isn't safe."

"It's safer outside of my car."

Officer Wheeler's talkie crackles and a voice says something Victor doesn't understand.

Victor scans him. "You should use that thing to call in a few ambulances and fire trucks."

"Excuse me?"

Another stream of traffic passes them. It's filled with trucks, SUVs and sedans. A baby blue beetle passes them. It's nearly the exact same color as the 37 Ford Coupe.

"600." Victor exhaled and reached for his clipboard on the passenger seat. The contract, everything he needed, was tightly packed under the clip. He climbed out of the work truck. His eyes locked on to the beautiful car as he walked toward the front steps.

It mystified him how it was so perfectly intact despite the humidity and twenty-six winters. The hood, roof and trunk of the car showed no signs of fading or rust. It took conscious effort to pull his attention from the car and turn toward the faded red front door.

He lifted his hand to knock just as the door opened. June stood on the threshold. She wore a brown dress with purple polka dots. Her smile glowed, and happiness seemed to emanate from her. Victor had never met a girl like her.

"Victor Crawford from the Federal Highway Administration, won't you come inside?" She held out her hand to welcome him.

This time, he took his fedora off and greeted her, "Ma'am."

She giggled.

As Victor passed her and stepped into the house, he got his first relief from the putrid smell of the swamp. She smelled like lavender and honey. He closed his eyes and inhaled as deeply as he could. When he opened his eyes, he had walked into the foyer.

The floors and walls were all oak with faded gray whitewash. Over the years, gaps had formed in the planks of wood that constituted the walls. There was an earthy brown dust on everything. A vine of some ivy was growing up from the cracks in the floor and around the front door. The vines snaked in and out of the gaps in the wood panels.

A stairway led upstairs. Its railing had strange ivy growing up it as well. Matted red carpet was tacked to each step, and at the top of the steps was a giant window with warped blown glass.

To Victor, the house felt eerie. It was an image out of a book, a run-down logger cabin, or a place no one should be living. He hadn't expected to see a home like this, not with someone so beautiful calling it home.

"Can I take your hat?" June held out her thin pink palm. That smile was still plastered on her face. Her blue eyes glowed.

"I should hold on to it, or I will certainly forget it."

Without a word, she passed him and stepped into the next room. Victor followed. Light, nearly twice as strong as that outside, shown from modest oil lamps and candles spread across the living room. Specks of dust floated around flickering flames. The walls were lined with shelves of leather-bound books. Green ivy had worked its way around them. Vines hung down from the tall ceilings.

Amongst the books were all sorts of honeys, oils and herbs in mason jars, each sealed tight. Something about the room churned an uneasy feeling in Victor's stomach.

"Have a seat." She pointed to an old whitewashed wooden bench behind him. It creaked as he tried to get comfortable. She sat in a rocker opposite him. "I can tell by your open stare that you think my house is a little queer, don't you?" She held her smile but her eyes narrowed.

"It's…different…"

She burst into laughter. "True…that is true…I'm not silly you know."

"I didn't accuse you of being so."

"No." She pointed to his face. "But your eyes…" Her petite hand waved around a bit. "They gave you away."

"I'm sorry."

"It's okay." Her arms spread out to draw his attention to the shelves. "I blend my own perfumes and work with fine oils. You'd be surprised what beautiful things grow in a swamp. I can't get electricity all the way out here but that doesn't matter, oil and candles work just fine."

The entire place felt odd and he couldn't stare at her long without getting dizzy. He anxiously chortled as he shifted papers on the clipboard.

In that moment, there was a low, barely audible whisper in his left ear, "*The baby smiled and cooed the entire time.*" It sounded like echoes from a far off room.

Victor startled, "What was that…is someone here?" He looked out the nearest window. Tendrils of leafless willow hung outside. The warped glass made their sway in the window look distorted and alive.

"Just you and me." Her smile didn't waver. "You're trying to change the subject." She crossed her legs and leaned back into the chair, with her arms laid out on the armrests. "You're very jumpy."

"It's just…" The willow continued to sway. A few branches scratched the window.

Her warm touch on his hand brought his attention back to her. "Don't let the swamp scare you."

"I'm not."

She leaned back again and crossed her arms. "If you want to buy this land, you can't be afraid of it."

"I don't...I don't want to buy it all...just a portion." Victor, allowing his job and his rehearsal of these conversations to take over, spun the clipboard around. "Our files say you own six square miles of land where we'd like to run the interstate highway. Are you familiar with Eisenhower's Federal-Aid Highway Act of 1956?"

"No sir." She shook her head.

Victor found himself launching into his trained salesman smile. "Well essentially, the state and federal government are making it easier for automobiles to get around." He pulled a stack of papers from his clipboard and held it out.

"Oh..." She scanned it. "Sweets...I don't want to read that."

"Well if you sign...you'll need to have it...I'm legally obligated to give it to you..." He held it in the air between them.

Her eyes shifted to the empty spot on the bench, next to Victor. "Set it there. I'll take a look at it later."

Victor set it down next to him. "I will say, I haven't encountered many people with as much land as you have, not in this area."

"My family was one of the first off the Mayflower. But the land they seized became a swampland. No one wants to buy a bog."

"So you've tried to sell it?"

"No." Her smile returned and she rocked. "You want me to sell it?"

"Not all of it." He leaned forward and held out the clipboard. A map of the swamp was sketched on top, with a red line scribed through the edge of it. "We'd just need about three miles and an anchorage on either side of this line."

June leaned forward. Her perfume impregnated his nose again, the same lavender and honey. "That's awfully close to my house."

"It is…but you'd still have a half a mile between you and the highway."

"Can we make it a quarter?"

"You want it closer?"

Her eyes focused onto a corner of the room high above Victor's head. "Maybe…I think a half mile will work." She perked up and scooted the rocking chair closer. "Where do I sign?"

"Seriously?"

"Seriously." She held out her hands.

Victor chuckled in disbelief. "That's got to be the easiest sell yet. You don't even want to know how much?"

"Are you writing me a check today?"

"No." Victor handed her the paperwork.

"Then I trust that you won't cheat me." She winked and took the pen. "Sign on the 'X's?"

"Yeah." Victor nodded and slid in closer. "You smell…amazing…"

"Thank you."

The perfume and the successful deal had Victor on a high. He stretched out his arms and leaned back in the chair. He looked out the window, and again noticed the Ford under the weeping willow. "Your car is beautiful, perfectly preserved. I haven't seen one that nice…well…not ever…only in pictures."

"Preserved?" She giggled and looked up at him. Some hair covered her bright blue eyes. "That's a good word for it. Like this house, I've kept the car the same way it was when I received them. This house was my mother's before she passed and the car was…from an acquaintance." She returned her attention to the paper. "Call it one of my talents, breathing life into old things."

Officer Wheeler steps closer to Victor. "Say that again."

"You need to call in some emergency personnel," Victor says. He continues to lean on his cane, hands folded over the top. "There's going to be an accident."

"And you know this, how?" Officer Wheeler furrows his brow.

Victor chuckles. "Are you inferring I'm causing the accident?"

"You seem pretty confident in your statement."

"Look at me…" He pushes off his cane as best he can. "I'm barely able to walk. Arthritis has started gnarling my fingers and toes. What can I do?"

"Jump…" As he says this, the officer gently cups his hand around Victor's elbow.

This sends a new wave of amusement through Victor. "I'm not going to jump." He points toward the oncoming traffic. "Watch…you'll see…it happens every ten years. Ever since we paved it the first time."

"I think you need to come with me."

"You think I'm a crazy old man."

"I didn't say that."

Victor's arm retracts. "You should."

There is a shriek of tires but the density of the swamp muffles it, like a scream into a pillow. Officer Wheeler turns around in time to watch a semi churn smoke into the air. Its front rim digs into the asphalt. Sparks trail out and into the air around it.

An unknowing SUV drives up to pass. It swerves, the motion of the vehicles frantic. The semi's nose drives into the neighboring SUV. The trailer fishtails around and the semi begins to flip. The cars following close behind crash into the bed. Pops and explosions vibrate the thick swamp air around them.

Tires, halting to a stop, continue to rattle Officer Wheeler and Victor. A red SUV clips the edge of the original semi's trailer and spins in a circle off the shoulder and toward the swamp.

Officer Wheeler covers his head and cries, "Oh my God."

Victor watched June the entire time she had been filling out the paperwork. Each stroke of her initials or signature sent a warm buzz through his body. He had fallen in love before; it felt the same, but not as strong.

"Are you still watching me?" Her eyes looked up at him as her face stayed downturned.

"I'm sorry ma'am." Victor coughed.

She flipped to the last few pages and a pit formed in Victor's stomach. They were nearly through. He didn't want this to end.

"I'm surprised the locals didn't scare you out of buying my land."

"Why would they do that?"

Her ballerina pen stroked across another dotted line. "They say my land is haunted."

"I can't tell you how many haunted homes and cities I've been to." The statement belied his intuition. There was something peculiar about the place, something haunting but at the same time warm and comforting. He never imagined haunting to be so coolly unnerving. His attention returned to the window and the skeletal fingers of the willow.

Whispers mounted. They matched the rhythm of the willow scratching. Each word lost in the crowd of another as if they were different voices talking at once. To Victor, they had to be the wind passing through the spaces between the wall planks. They had to be the rustling of tree branches. It was too unnerving to think of it being anything else.

"So you didn't hear the story?" Her big blue eyes looked up at him and he whipped his attention back to her. "They say, back in 1666, this area was fertile farmland with a cute pond in the middle."

Victor relaxed his arms and did his best to push the anxieties back down into his gut. He made an effort to hang on every word, every movement of her perfect pink lips. "And your family owned it before it became a swamp?"

"Not exactly." Her soothing tone hid the whispers even as her attention shifted back to her paperwork. "The settlers here were Puritans. While they have generally unfairly received a bad name, this particular group was in fact zealous and paranoid. On June sixth, in 1666, a baby was born to a widow far past her prime—sixty."

Victor shook his head. "That's not possible."

She pointed with the pen, "And that's why this is only a legend." She grinned. "The old lady had always wanted a child, so you can imagine, when a husbandless old woman turns up pregnant, the superstitious town blamed witchcraft."

A cold breeze blew against Victor's neck. Something like a murmur tickled his ear. A word was spoken but he couldn't discern it from the hiss of wind through the walls and the rasping on the window. He blinked and focused on June, her beauty, and her eyes as she spoke.

"The night of the baby's birth, June sixth, the townsfolk broke into the widow's home and snatched the newborn out of the mother's arms. They took that poor baby all the way to the cute little pond and tossed her." June looked up from the paperwork, slid the pen into the clip, and held it out to Victor.

He received it, swallowed hard, and asked, "What happened to the baby?"

"What happens to all newborns tossed into water…" She stopped smiling. "She drowned. The widow became a recluse and hid from the murderers. She moved farther away from the town. The townsfolk spread rumors about the baby and the mother."

The cold breeze wafted over Victor again. The whispers became discernable and united in one voice, "*We should have killed the mother.*" Victor jolted out of his chair. The hat fell from his lap and tumbled to the ground. Dust kicked up around it.

"Are you okay?"

"I…" He wildly looked around the room. The grayness of the day outside did not match the bright yellow glow of the inside. The ivy, the car, and this girl, June, did not coalesce. Victor ran his hands up and down his thighs as he stared at her. Fear locked his knees and planted his heels.

She stood. Worry marked her countenance. "You're white as a sheet." She placed her hand on his shoulder. "I haven't scared you, have I?" Her body filled the space between them and brushed against his.

"I'm okay…just thought I heard something…" Victor tried to act confident, even though he felt the opposite. Her warm touch removed the chill from the back of his neck. He decided, to show he wasn't scared, to ask further, "And the land twisted into a swamp because of the death?"

June chuckled. "No. Damming up north did. That and digging broke open a number of underground streams. This area became a swamp because of colonization."

"What about the story? What happened to the townsfolk and the mother?" Victor bent over and picked up his hat. His hand shook the entire way down and when he stood, it took all his concentration to place it on his head.

June let go of Victor's shoulder and stepped away from him. "Ten years of rumors had turned the town into a bloodthirsty horde. Every illness, calamity, or drought felt by the town was blamed on the widow and her dead child. On the anniversary of the baby's death, the vicar that had rallied the village to kill the baby rallied it to kill the mother."

"Wait..." Victor leaned on the corner of his seat. "Why didn't they kill the mother with the baby? Why did they wait ten years?"

She smiled, ran a finger across his jawline, and replied, "It's a legend, a story. I don't know why they waited ten years. The point is that the widow became a recluse, that she shut herself off from the world. So they found her house outside of the town, dragged her out to the front yard, and stabbed her through the chest."

She rested her hand on her hip. "That's when they heard the screams of a ten-year-old girl. All eyes locked onto the girl at the front door and they knew that this widow, this witch, had somehow brought her daughter up from the depths of the swamp and given her life. Every last one died when the scream stopped ringing in their ears."

A silence hung over the room while her words found purchase.

"I like it." Victor focused on her lips. He was comforted by her image. The scariness of this entire place was lost in that smile, lost in the warmth of her touch and the smell of her perfume. A strange urge to kiss her overwhelmed him and weakened his knees. "I still don't get why they waited ten years."

"Some fear takes a while to grow." She stood, rounded her chair, and fished a bottle off the shelf. June returned with a jar and held it out to Victor.

"What's this?"

"My perfume. I can tell you like it." She lifted the jar in front of his face. "It's a recipe older than you or me." That same intoxicating smile washed over her face.

Victor received the gift. "Thank you." He rolled the jar, with a suspended piece of dark purple lavender inside, between his hands. "I think..."

He looked up from the bottle and into her blue eyes, "I think the townsfolk loved the widow, or maybe her husband. It was easier for them to kill a newborn than to kill someone they shared memories, a life with. It took ten years of the widow not in their lives to cleave the memories, to build enough terror needed to hate."

"Could be." She put her hand on his chest. "I like it. I think I'll use it the next time I tell the story."

Despite the conflicting emotions of fear and love, Victor asked, "Are you that girl?"

June laughed. "It's a legend, Victor." She stepped up on her toes and kissed him on the cheek. Her lips seemed to burn his skin. She whispered, "Fear is born a minute apart from love."

Smoke rises from the wreckage. Officer Wheeler grips Victor's arm. "Stay put. Don't move an inch." He clicks on his microphone and says, "We've got a pileup on twenty-four…" His tone grows in intensity as he lets go, turns, and rushes toward the accident. "We'll need life flight," is the last discernable thing Victor can hear.

A sigh escapes Victor. His old eyes try to see what is going on inside the heap of twisted metal. As far as he can tell, there isn't much. Already, the smell of gasoline and oil compete with the putrid smell of the swamp.

His hips begin to lock up and a jabbing pain grips his body. "It happens every ten years. Why didn't I notice until now?"

A cold breeze brushes his neck. It carries a whisper of voices, the words of which he can't discern, and the smell of lavender and honey. He smiles and a jolt of energy courses through him.

Turning toward the breeze, he can see her out of the corner of his eye. June stands just a few feet away in a brown dress with purple polka dots. Her long black hair is tied up to show her pale face. A smile curves her pink lips and her blue eyes glow with that same happiness they did all those years ago.

"You're here?" Victor asks.

"Every ten years."

Victor takes a deep breath. "I haven't smelled that perfume in nearly fifty years."

"It has been a long time." She steps closer. "Why are you here, Victor?"

"And you…" he stands as upright as his knotted spine will allow him, "you haven't aged a day."

"Thanks to you."

Sirens from oncoming emergency vehicles distract Victor for a moment, but he returns to her. "I'm dying."

"I can see that." She looks him over and says, "I remember that boy who visited me all those years ago. He was so young and handsome and nearly insulted me with his obsession over a blue Ford Coupe instead of me."

"I was trying to be polite." He smiles and he feels as if they are old friends catching up on time lost. "Can you help?"

June watches her bare feet as she walks over to him. She places her pink palm on his chest. "Why would I?"

"You fell in love with me the day you met me. I know you did… that's why I'm still alive, that's why you gave me the perfume. Like that car, you somehow preserved me, and yourself…kept me alive longer than I should be."

"That sounds like a legend, Victor…" Her expression becomes playful. Her hand slides down his chest and to his hand. "Are you sure I love you?"

"You've haunted me every day of my life since we met. As my life grew and changed, that image of you when we first met has always been there. June, I fell in love with you the minute I saw you."

She turns her back to him and begins to lead him toward the swamp. "We'll need a bigger accident if you're going to stay with me. I need you young and handsome again."

Behind them, more tires scream. Metal crashes into metal. Officer Wheeler yells. There is a pop and explosion which displaces the thick swamp air around them.

DENIAL

Ralph Uttaro

It was past midnight, probably closer to two o'clock. The moon cast a phosphorescent glow over the gravel at my feet, the air was heavy and slick with dew, the snapping of crickets echoed around me. There was rustling in the brush on the other side of the road. I felt a pair of amber eyes surveilling me.

I had been standing on the shoulder of the two-lane county road for what seemed like an hour, but hadn't seen a single car pass in either direction. I figured I might be there until the sun came up. I stared at the row of *Ford/Dole '76* lawn signs planted in the grass. The President's big-toothed smile seemed forced, reproachful. I wondered whether Mallory even knew I was gone.

A splash of light spread across the pavement then crawled upward to illuminate the trees. I heard the low roar of an engine and a cream-colored Galaxie convertible appeared over a rise in the road, its high-beams hazy white in the fog that hovered near the ground. The driver's long hair trailed in the wind as she flew by me then suddenly hit the brakes. A hint of rubber mixed with the musky air as the car fishtailed to a stop about sixty yards down the road. The driver shifted into park and revved the engine as I ran and tossed my duffel bag into the back seat.

"Where you going?" She was about my age, had dark hair, a long sullen face, wet pouty lips.

"New Jersey."

"I can take you there."

"That's gotta be two hundred miles."

"I don't care. I'll take you anywhere you want to go." She looked over at me. Her eyes were glazed, her speech thick and slow. She was stoned.

She pushed the accelerator down hard and we took off. We hit the first curve at full speed, the tires making a rippling sound as they dug into the pavement to take the corner. My hand pressed against the dashboard.

"I'm Joanie," she said, her voice rising to be heard above the road noise.

"Mike," I replied. Then there was silence.

Mallory would eventually wonder where I had gone, worry that I had just vanished in the night. If the Galaxie ended up wrapped around a tree, she would regret it for the rest of her life, but there wasn't anything she could do about it. She wouldn't dare call my house. My mother had met Mallory only once, at parents' weekend, but had made it clear to me that she didn't like her.

"She puts on airs," she told me. "We're just simple people. We don't do like that."

Joanie was looking straight ahead now, both hands tightly gripping the top of the steering wheel, her shoulders hunched slightly forward. She wasn't pretty. A thick crescent of skin curved around the bottom of her chin, her eyes were small and set too close together, her nose was wide and flat. Her body was another story. She was wearing a snug orange halter top, her brown legs glistened in the moonlight. I noticed for the first time that she was barefoot.

"What are you doing out here anyway?" she asked after a minute or two. "I mean, hitchhiking in the middle of the night?"

"It's a long story. I'm too tired to get into it."

"Suit yourself." She shrugged.

§

I had flown up to Syracuse on Thursday night. I hadn't seen Mallory since final exam week in the middle of May. We had stayed in touch by mail, had spoken on the phone only twice and even then only briefly. Long-distance was expensive. Forty-eight long days. I was ready to explode, but when she met me at the airport all she gave me was a weak, dry kiss.

"What's wrong?" I tried not to sound irritated.

"Nothing. I need to get the car back. My sister has summer school tonight."

She seemed to relax a bit while we waited at baggage claim. She held my hand loosely as we walked to the car. I took a deep breath, told myself that we just needed to get readjusted to each other. As we pulled out onto Route 81, I asked her if the plan for the weekend was all set.

"Billy Grimes called last night," she said. "There's a big folk music festival in the Catskills. He's going with Jack and Katie."

"So?"

"I told him we would go."

Billy Grimes and Jack Valenti were music majors. Katie was Jack's girlfriend. They all lived in the Syracuse area like Mallory but all in different towns. Mallory first met the three of them in an Intro to Poetry class. Billy and Jack played together at coffeehouses and bars down in The Commons: "City of New Orleans," "Lyin' Eyes," "Tangled Up In Blue," a couple of tinny ballads they had composed themselves. They were slackers.

Billy was pale and gangly, a patchy beard covering parts of his face; his clothes always smelled of stale cigarettes. He was a hound. I had seen him in action around campus. Jack was sarcastic, condescending, dark-skinned, jittery. Katie was a head taller than him, a sixties flower child. I didn't know what Mallory saw in them. Mallory mentioned in one of her letters that she had been hanging around with them a lot. She said that Billy had written a couple of new songs that were pretty good.

"I thought we were going to do the wineries?" I said. We had crafted a plan in our exchange of letters earlier in the summer. We would commandeer one of her parents' cars and drive down to the Finger Lakes—the drinking age was still eighteen back then. We would hit the winery trail then find a motel room for the night. We would tell her parents that her college roommate was having a party in Elmira and that we were going to spend the night there. As the weeks passed, Mallory's letters got shorter and less frequent, but I made my plane reservations anyway.

"We can do the wineries next time. This concert is huge, like another Woodstock. It'll be a great time. Jack knows a place where we can camp for free. The concert starts Saturday morning. We're going to drive down tomorrow."

She turned to look at me. I knew that expression. She had already made up her mind.

Mallory's parents took us to the country club for dinner. Mallory was irritable, correcting me for using the wrong fork, rolling her eyes when I asked her mother what escargot was (I pronounced it wrong too). Mallory did nothing to carry the conversation. There were long uncomfortable silences. Her parents eventually ignored us and started talking about the club tournament that was coming up the following weekend. When we got back to her house, Mallory turned on the television and curled herself up in a corner of the big sectional in the family room. When I tried to move in closer she hissed, "I don't feel comfortable with my parents around."

"You sure there isn't something wrong?" I asked in the morning. I was sitting in the kitchen, Mallory was staring into the open refrigerator. She took out a carton of orange juice and set it down on the table in front of me next to an empty glass.

"I'm getting in the shower," she said, then went upstairs.

They picked us up a little past noon in Jack's primer-gray GTO. We had dug up a tent and two sleeping bags from Mallory's basement. Billy was sitting in the back seat on the passenger side behind Katie. Mallory and I put our gear in the trunk and walked around to the driver's side. She was only five-foot-two but she insisted on taking the window seat.

"I'm claustrophobic," she said. "You know I can't sit in the middle for four hours."

I folded myself into the back of the car and settled one foot on either side of the hump that covered the transmission. Jack's stripped-down muscle car didn't have air conditioning so the windows were all open. Billy fell asleep five minutes after we got on the road, his head rolling sideways against the window opening, his long hair fluttering in the wind. Thick humid air rippled across my face, the back of my shirt quickly got soaked and stuck to the black vinyl seat. My thighs were cramping, but every time I moved and brushed against Mallory's leg she pushed me away.

§

I first met Mallory at freshman orientation the previous August. She had long straight blonde hair and incongruously thick, dark eyebrows. Her face was small, round, her green eyes flecked with shards of brown that glinted like broken glass in the sun. She had firm athletic legs although I never once saw her exercise. There weren't many girls back home in Teaneck that looked that good, and if there were they weren't interested in me.

I saw her at the campus rathskeller a few days later. To my surprise, she motioned for me to sit down. The other girls at the table were dressed in jeans; Mallory wore tailored white slacks and a tight black blouse. Her lips were outlined in a moist, subtle pink lipstick. She slid her chair over and locked in on me like there was no one else at the table. She told me that her father was a surgeon, that they lived along the seventh hole of a country club, had a summer place on some lake with a long Indian name—she acted like I should have heard of it. We bought a six-pack to go and ended up in her room, half undressed and making out when her roommate walked in on us.

We started spending most of our time together. She seemed to like the stories I told her about growing up in Teaneck. She seemed impressed that I would just hop on a bus with my friends and go into the city to catch a Yankees game or hang out in the Village. I took liberties, telling her about a concert at Madison Square Garden that I never attended, a mugging on a subway platform that I never witnessed. She laughed when I told her about Sunday dinners at my grandmother's house, sometimes twenty people crammed into the little dining room eating spaghetti with red sauce, meatballs, braciole.

"What's a braciole?" The word sounded foreign coming out of her mouth.

"It's this piece of meat that's rolled up with all this stuff inside. Cheese, raisins, pine nuts. They stick a toothpick through it to hold it all together."

"I can't imagine that many people at dinner."

"It's pretty crazy." I laughed.

"I always had this idea of what people from New Jersey were like. I thought they were all so rough and loud. You know, real aggressive. But you're different. You're just a sweet guy."

I couldn't believe my good luck. I wrote to my high school buddy Jimmy. He always said he liked his women "short, blonde and built" although he never dated anyone that looked like that. I reported that Mallory met his criteria. She was easily one of the four or five hottest girls in our freshman class. She was sophisticated, confident, funny. The truth was that I didn't think I deserved her.

§

"We're here," Jack said brightly as he pulled the GTO into a small gravel parking lot. The rest of us looked around skeptically. We were on the edge of a narrow road with nothing but trees on either side. We followed Jack down a path into the woods. There was a clearing with a circle of rocks surrounding a pile of dusty ashes and chunks of partially burned wood. It looked like someone had camped there recently. There was no running water, not even an outhouse in sight.

"How did you find this place?" Mallory asked.

"I grew up near here. My grandfather still lives down the road. We used to run around here all the time when I was a kid."

"Cool," she replied.

Jack began to assemble the tent he had brought. Mallory disappeared into the woods with Billy and Katie to collect kindling and logs for our fire, leaving me to put our tent together. I had never been camping before. I hammered the four metal stakes into the ground just like Jack had done. I fumbled with the poles, tried to pull the twisted blue nylon taut and stretch the tie lines to the stakes. I couldn't get the lines tight. Mallory and Billy and Katie came back and dumped their loads of wood in the circle. Mallory glared at our sagging, lopsided tent.

Billy laughed. He had announced earlier that he was going to sleep under the stars.

"Here, let me help you with that," he said.

"Good idea," Mallory replied. She bent down to untie a line from one of the stakes.

"Jack is going into town to get some ice," Katie said. "You guys need anything?"

"I'm good," Billy answered.

"Why don't you go with him, Mike," Mallory said to me. "He could probably use a hand. I think you can manage that."

As Jack and I headed off toward the car, Katie called after us. "Get some more beer too."

Jack fiddled with the AM radio. There was a religious station with a clear signal, an easy listening station like WVNJ that was always on in the kitchen back home, a country station that faded in and out. In between, there was a whole lot of static. When he came around to the country station for the third time, Jack turned the power off in disgust. We drove quietly for a few minutes. I wasn't in the mood to be sociable.

"Man, Mallory was right," Jack said suddenly. "You're really up-tight." The air went out of my lungs. "What are you *doing* here anyway?"

"Doing?"

"Like, this trip. Why are you here, man?"

"Mallory asked me."

"She did?"

"We've been planning it for weeks."

He shrugged. "If you say so. It's kind of awkward, though. I thought it was just going to be the four of us."

§

It was more than awkward. If it was just awkward I would never have found myself speeding down a dark country road in the middle of the night with a strange, stoned girl behind the wheel. Joanie floored the Galaxie as we climbed a hill, and when we hit the crest we went airborne for a beat or two. I should have been scared but instead I felt a rush, a weird sense of adventure. The tape deck was cranked up to full volume—*The Doors Greatest Hits*. Jim Morrison was singing "Touch Me" and Joanie was singing along, her voice harsh, loud, terribly off-key. Every time it came to the chorus ("c'mon, c'mon, c'mon, c'mon, now touch me babe"), she would reach over and squeeze my thigh.

Twenty minutes later, she eased off the accelerator and the Galaxie drifted onto the shoulder. She turned into a long narrow driveway and dialed down the volume on the music. A dog charged at the car barking, then backed away slowly. As we bumped over the rutted gravel, a mobile home came into view off to the right. There was a rickety picnic table near the door and a rusted blue Impala parked on the grass in front.

"What are we doing?" I asked.

"We'll get some sleep, then I'll take you to Jersey in the morning."

"You don't have to do that."

"I know." She got out of the car. I followed her.

The screen door creaked as she pulled it back. The front door behind it was wide open. The place smelled of mildew, stale cigar smoke, cat piss. We entered what looked in the dark to be a living room. I could see the outlines of a big console television on the far wall, could hear someone snoring on a sofa. She led me down a narrow passageway. Her hand was as damp and clammy as the air.

Joanie pulled me into a bedroom and began to unfasten the button on my shorts. When she pulled the zipper down, they slid to the floor. I yanked her halter top over her head and we tumbled onto the bed, the box spring under the thin mattress thumping against the wall. Her breath reeked, both our bodies were ripe with perspiration. I slid down and wrestled with her cutoff jeans, struggling to slide them over her hips.

It was almost dawn when I skulked out of the trailer. It was light enough to see that the person snoring on the sofa was a bearded middle-aged man. He wore only boxer shorts and his belly rose and fell with each shallow breath. I opened the screen door slowly but the hinges creaked anyway. The front steps groaned under my weight. The dog was lying in the yard. He lifted his head and growled softly as I stepped past him, finally yawning and laying his head back down.

To my surprise, a brown pickup stopped as soon as I emerged at the end of the driveway. The driver was a tall, dour woman with a small head and rust colored hair curled in a tight perm. She wore a green and white gingham dress and smelled like talcum powder.

"They say you ain't supposed to pick up hitchhikers but you look clean enough. Besides, the good book tells us we should be the good Samaritan."

"Thank you." My mouth was so dry I could barely get the words out.

"Well, I'm only going over near to Kingston to visit with my sister. She just got out of the hospital. Got her gallbladder out."

"That's fine. Perfect," I said. I was grateful just to get out of there.

She left me at an all-night diner on Route 9W where I decided to have breakfast. I caught a series of short rides after that, and was dropped off in towns I had never heard of—Ulster Park and Milton and Middle Hope. There were long stretches in between, standing by the side of the road, drivers averting their eyes as they passed. It was almost noon before I made it to Highland Falls where a trucker picked me up and took me all the way down to Paramus.

I called my friend Jimmy from a pay phone and he agreed to pick me up. His family was at the shore for the weekend so he said I could spend the night on his sofa. That way I wouldn't have to explain to my parents why I was back so soon. We stopped to pick up a six-pack then settled down in his backyard. I told him the whole story, every agonizing detail.

§

The sun was going down when Jack and I got back from the store. A fire was burning in the stone circle. Mallory's tent was standing straight and tight. She was sitting on a blanket facing Billy, the two of them absorbed in conversation. We grilled hot dogs over the fire on long sticks, the casings bursting from the heat, the juice sizzling as it dropped into the flames. We heated up a couple of cans of pork and beans and took turns eating out of the pot. We washed it all down with six-packs of Miller.

Jack and Billy each grabbed a flashlight and trekked back to the car to get their guitars. Katie reached into her backpack and pulled out a foil packet loaded with fat, tightly rolled joints. She selected one wrapped in a bright pink rolling paper and lit up. When she handed it to me, I took a long draw and held it in, the smoke burning my nose and lungs until I finally exhaled.

"Go easy there camper, the pink ones are laced with hash," Katie said.

"No problem."

I inhaled deeply again and held on to the joint. I wanted to show that I could keep up with them. I never partied in high school, afraid it would start me down the road toward other things. I had seen too many junkies on street corners, strung out after shooting heroin or sniffing too much glue. At first Mallory thought my abstinence was quaint, but soon it became a point of contention. She wasn't going to stop. I would find myself sitting alone at a party while she was across the room getting high. Eventually I gave in. She seemed pleased the first night I tried it, giggling when I told her I was starving. "Mikey's got the munchies," she'd announced giddily.

Katie lit another joint and passed it to Billy. He held it up to Mallory's lips. She tilted her head up and to one side and released a column of smoke into the darkness. Billy passed the joint to Katie then started strumming a song I had never heard before, a loosely arranged set of simple chords. Probably one of the tunes he had written. To my surprise, Mallory began singing. I had never heard her sing before. Her voice was thin and timid. Billy encouraged her with his eyes, a smile, a gentle bobbing of his chin. When the song ended, Billy began to clap softly; Jack and Katie laughed and joined in. I felt invisible.

The joint had burned down to a tiny roach, which I pinched between my fingers. I sucked in the dregs. I had smoked the whole thing myself. I must have drifted off to sleep shortly after that. When I woke up I was in the tent. The sleeping bag next to me was empty. I didn't hear a guitar. There was no singing, no voices at all. I crawled to the head of the tent and softly pulled back the flap. The fire had burned down to a pile of smoldering orange and gray embers. A sleeping bag was barely visible in the grass, downhill a few yards beyond the fire. I could see gentle movement in the moonlight, could hear the soft rustling of nylon, the unmistakable sound of Mallory's rhythmic sighing.

§

"So he was banging her right there?" Jimmy crushed the can of Bud in his hand. "Are you kidding me? What, she was trying to rub your nose in it?"

"The crazy thing is, I still love her."

"No you don't," Jimmy barked. "No fucking way. If she even tries to call you, you ain't home."

She never called. I sat in my bedroom and tortured myself thinking about Mallory and Billy in his sleeping bag in the grass by the campfire. I imagined them doing it in the back seat of her parents' car, quietly on the shag carpet in her finished basement while the rest of the family watched television upstairs, in the middle of the seventh fairway under a full moon. It tore me up. I waited anxiously for the mail every day. Nothing.

"Don't you call her, you hear?" Jimmy would tell me every night. After two weeks I couldn't stand it any longer.

Her mother answered the phone. "She's not here." She hung up without saying anything more.

I started to think about what it would be like when I got back to school. People would find out right away that Mallory was with Billy. I would wonder how much of the story had gotten out. I would worry that everyone was talking behind my back, laughing at me. All our friends would probably take her side. It would be humiliating.

I practiced what I would say to Mallory the first time I saw her. I would tell her that I felt nothing, that I had gone on a wild ride that night and had sex with a total stranger, had been over her before dawn. But none of that was true. I wasn't close to being over Mallory. And nothing really happened in Joanie's squalid trailer that night. By the time I pulled her pants down over her feet, I realized she was sound asleep.

§

I didn't have to wait long. It was the day after my parents drove me back to school. I was heading across the quad toward the book store when I saw Mallory and Billy. They stopped. Mallory said something to Billy. He shrugged and lit a cigarette while she continued down the sidewalk in my direction. Her look had changed. A thick ponytail sprouted straight out from the back of her head. She wasn't wearing any makeup. She wore tight, cut-off dungarees that were fraying at the knees, a loose white T-shirt without a bra. She had never looked so good. She was looking down at the sidewalk. Over her shoulder, I could see Billy watching her, a smirk on his face.

She wrapped her arms around my neck. I didn't know what to do.

"It's so good to see you, Mike." She pushed back and placed her hands on my shoulders. The speech I had rehearsed dissolved in my brain. I stared, blinked, cleared my throat. "How are you?" She looked up at me with a patronizing smile.

"How do you think I am?" My voice broke.

"Michael. Don't..."

"Why didn't you tell me?"

"I'm sorry for the way it happened. Let's just leave it at that, okay?"

It wasn't much of an apology. Her eyes showed no remorse, no emotion at all really. I guess she just wanted closure. As I watched her walk away with Billy, I wondered how I ever thought I could be in love with someone like that.

Jimmy tried to tell me. He insisted that a girl like Mallory just wasn't for me. He said I should forget about her and all those other high-class college bitches, that I should come home and find myself a good Jersey girl. Maybe Jimmy was right.

THE SCREAMING BRIDGE

Chris Burnside

Tabitha clutched the wheel with both hands as she navigated her Prius through the darkness of I-70 West. "I'm never going back there. I'll send for my things."

"Don't you think that's a tad extreme, Tabby?" Jason's voice came through the car's speakers, transmitted from the phone beside her. Her brother had always been the more carefree of the pair. His everything-will-be-fine attitude only made her grip the steering wheel tighter.

"I don't. And neither would you if you saw what happened."

"Look, I'm not saying it didn't happen, but—"

"The clock bled, Jason!"

"Rachel's going to wake up if you keep yelling."

Tabitha looked into the rearview mirror, angling her neck so she could see her daughter sleeping in her car seat.

"She's still asleep. And that's not the point. The clock bled. Those three words should never be said in succession. Clocks do not bleed."

"Exactly—clocks don't bleed. Probably a busted water pipe in the wall behind it."

"The water in my house is not red. And all three hands were on six."

"Six is the one that points down. If the hands broke, that's where they would point." His justifications were infuriatingly calm.

"Rachel's old walker was rolling back and forth across the floor. By itself."

"Could have been the house settling."

"Are you listening to yourself, Jason? Rachel is three years old. Her walker was in the basement closet for the last two years. Who put it in the living room?"

"Look, Tabby, I'll admit that it's a little weird—"

"Yes, and Albert Einstein is mildly intelligent."

"—but there's a rational explanation. Your house is not haunted."

"This is where we agree, big brother. It's not the house that's haunted. This has been happening to me since we were little."

"No inanimate object in Mom and Dad's house ever bled."

"No, it was always little things. Doors opening and closing by themselves. Strange noises."

"It was an old house, Tabby. That's all."

She continued as if he hadn't spoken. "But it's gotten way worse the last few years, ever since Rachel was born. My phone will ring and show 'unknown caller.' And there's no one on the other end."

Jason sighed. "You're just taking things that happen to everyone and ascribing magical significance to them."

"Bleeding clocks *are* magically significant. And what about the scratch marks that appeared on the inside of the basement door? I don't have a dog. Or a cat. Or mice. Don't you dare suggest mice. It's like something was trying to claw its way out of the basement."

"Maybe Rachel did it."

"She's three, jackass. She can't even reach the lock on the door."

"I don't want to argue with you, sis. If you say it happened, then it must have happened. How's she doing, anyway?"

"Rachel?" Tabitha stole another quick glance at her daughter. "Way better than I am."

"Kids are resilient," Jason assured her.

"You're not kidding. While I was screaming and grabbing the suitcase, she was drawing a picture. With crayons. Totally calm. She actually asked me if I was all right."

"Wow. What a sweetie."

"She is," Tabitha agreed, "which is why we are done with that house. I will not let anything happen to her."

"Regardless of what happened, you'll both be safe here."

"Are you sure Rob doesn't mind us staying?"

"Well, you know how he hates your face. But as long as you don't look at him..."

"Har har."

"We'd love for you to visit. Seriously. We don't get to see Rachel nearly enough. Dayton isn't that far from Columbus, you know."

"Don't guilt me, Jason. We'll be there in about an hour."

"Sounds good. Don't rush, though. Just chill and enjoy a peaceful drive."

"When have you ever known me to chill?"

"Good point. So grip that steering wheel at ten and two, grit your teeth, and adhere closely to the speed limit." Tabitha smiled as she noted how she was already following all three suggestions. "I love you, Tabby."

"Love you too, Jason. Bye." Tabitha thumbed the button on her steering wheel to disconnect the call. She forced herself to take a deep breath and looked back at Rachel again. She looked so peaceful with her head resting against the side of the car seat. So vulnerable.

Tabitha tried to take her brother's advice and remain calm. She tried not to think of how the clock's hands had twirled in asynchronous fashion before stopping on six, of how blood had poured from the numbers like the clock face wasn't a solid piece of plastic, of how the drywall nails had pushed back out of the wall and right through the wallpaper as if something in the wall had tried to force its way out.

"I'm a big girl," she said to herself. "I can survive one quiet hour alone with my thoughts."

Thirty seconds later, Tabitha switched on the car radio and turned the volume low. She flipped through her presets using the steering wheel's controls until she landed on NPR. It was a re-airing of an interview with a local author.

"And that's the scariest haunting you've ever experienced?" the interviewer asked.

"You've got to be kidding me," Tabitha said to the radio.

"Without a doubt," the author answered, his voice deep yet soft. "Green Lawn Abbey is filled with angry spirits." Tabitha knew this to be true. Her experiences had bred in her a fascination with spirits—Jason had once suggested that she major in ghost busting—she knew all the haunted houses, churches, prisons, bridges and roads in Ohio. Green Lawn Abbey was near the top of the list.

The author continued. "I've rarely encountered more than one spirit in a place. I guess you could say they don't get along. And the Abbey is packed with them, so you can imagine the chaos, spiritually speaking. Even regular people with no connection to the spirit world experience powerful emotions. As a medium, I could barely stay on my feet."

"It's that powerful?" the interviewer asked.

"The older the spirit, the more intense its presence, and Green Lawn Abbey has some old spirits."

"It seems appropriate that you're using this as the setting of your new book," the interviewer said. "Tell us about that."

Tabitha's thumb slid to the button that would advance to her next preset station.

"The book is called *Rachel is Mine*, and it will be out tonight."

Tabitha froze. He hadn't actually said that. He couldn't have.

"That's an intriguing title," the interviewer mused. "*Rachel is Mine*. What does it mean?" She hadn't misheard. A coincidence, then.

"It's about a woman," the author described, "a stupid, stupid bitch who thinks she can get away from me in a car. In a Prius."

"A Prius?" The interviewer laughed. "She must be stupid."

"She is. So very stupid. As if I'm stuck in that house. As if I'm not stuck to *her*. And she doesn't realize that Rachel is mine. Hence the title."

Chills numbed Tabitha's arms and legs. Every hair on her body stood on end. She could feel her heart pounding.

The interview continued. "What sort of book is it?"

"I suppose most people would call it horror. A dark and mighty spirit coming for a little girl, her stupid bitch mother in the way. But to me, it's really a love story. Two souls destined to be together."

Tabitha's eyes burned, and she realized she hadn't blinked for some time. She looked at the dashboard and saw that she was coasting along at thirty miles per hour. She'd been so transfixed that she didn't even remember the last few miles.

"Do you hear me, Tabitha?" the author asked.

Tabitha stared forward, afraid to even turn her head, afraid that something was in the car with her, just beyond her field of vision.

"I'm asking you a question." The car began to accelerate despite

Tabitha barely putting any pressure on the gas pedal. Tabitha took her foot off the gas, but the car continued to pick up speed. Forty miles per hour. Fifty. "Do you hear me, Tabitha?"

"Yes," she croaked, barely audible. Sixty. Tabitha applied the brakes. The car slowed for a moment before accelerating again. She pressed harder and heard the brakes grind uselessly.

"Why are you running, Tabitha? You're not even doing a good job of that. Shocking, I know. When's the last time you did anything right?" Seventy.

"This isn't happening," Tabitha whispered.

"You have a funny definition of *isn't*, you know? If you think this isn't happening, wait until you see what doesn't happen next." Eighty.

Tabitha gritted her teeth. "Leave us alone." Her voice was little more than a whisper, but it bristled with anger.

"Or what? You'll crash your car? Almost ninety miles an hour is quite reckless when you have a toddler in the back seat. You should really—" Tabitha punched the radio's power button, silencing the voice. The car ceased accelerating but continued at eighty-five miles per hour.

"You didn't really think that would work, did you?" the author asked, despite the radio being off. "Have you ever even seen a scary movie?"

"I've seen them all," Tabitha muttered. At this speed, even a slight grade in the road made it difficult for her to maintain control of the car.

"Not a quick study, are you?"

"What do you want?" she managed, pulling hard on the wheel as the car veered.

"You know."

"This is your plan, then? To kill us in a car crash?" The author did not respond. "How would that help your agenda?"

Tabitha was startled from her questions by flashing red and blue lights from behind her. The police car's siren whooped once. The Prius began to slow, and Tabitha quickly applied the brakes and guided it onto the shoulder. The police car, lights still flashing, pulled over behind the Prius.

"Mommy?"

Tabitha turned to look back at Rachel, completely forgetting her fear that something might be right next to her. The three-year-old was blinking groggily and looking around.

"Oh, Rachel. I'm sorry I woke you up."

"Are we at Uncle Jason's?"

"Not yet, baby." Tabitha looked in her side mirror and saw the highway patrolman approaching her car. "Mommy has to stop to talk to the police."

"Are we in trouble?" Rachel asked.

"Maybe just a little."

The patrolman stopped beside the back door of the car and shined a flashlight into the back seat. Rachel looked into the light and squinted. Tabitha watched, dumbfounded, as her daughter smiled and waved, so sweet and innocent.

The patrolman advanced to Tabitha's door, and she lowered the window for him. He shined the flashlight into her face. Tabitha winced at the bright light.

"Ma'am, normally I would ask if you knew how fast you were going. But seeing as you've got a little girl in the back seat, I have to assume that you had absolutely no idea."

"That's right, officer, I don't—"

"Furthermore, given those circumstances, I have to also assume that you've not had anything to drink tonight."

"No, I—"

"And I'm certain you must have somewhere very important to be at nearly midnight on a Tuesday evening. How am I doing with these assumptions?"

Tabitha waited a moment to see if the patrolman would cut her off again. "That's all correct, officer. I didn't know how fast I was going because I was distracted, and I don't drink, tonight or ever. We're heading to visit my brother in Dayton."

"Uncle Jason!" Rachel called from the back seat. Tabitha watched the officer for his reaction to Rachel's outburst. His face remained stoic, so she forced a smile.

"Awfully late for a visit," the patrolman said.

"We got held up. It's tough to pack for a three-year-old when that three-year-old is helping you pack." Tabitha again forced a smile.

"And you just got distracted while you were driving?"

"Yes, officer. I didn't realize my speed."

"What distracted you?" the patrolman probed.

Tabitha stared back, eyes wide despite the bright flashlight. Her mouth opened twice, and each time, she shut it without speaking.

"What distracted you?" the patrolman repeated. "Is there something you haven't told me?"

"Honestly, I don't know what to say. You would never believe me."

"Ma'am, considering that the reason might mean the difference between a warning and a citation, you might want to try to convince me."

Tabitha paused again. "Well, it started when we were at home earlier tonight, when the clock—"

The patrolman's radio sprayed static, interrupting her. "All units," the female dispatcher's voice called over the radio, "we have a two-zero-seven in progress on I-70 westbound."

"Ma'am?" the patrolman asked.

"Yes?"

"You were saying?"

"The victim is a three-year-old girl," the dispatcher said. "She's been kidnapped by her mother."

The patrolman watched Tabitha, seemingly oblivious to the radio. "Is something wrong, ma'am?" he asked. Tabitha realized her mouth was half-open and her hands were shaking. She hurriedly folded them in her lap.

"You don't know?" she asked.

"You haven't told me yet. Something about a clock."

The dispatcher crackled over the radio again. "The girl's father is desperate to get her back and away from her stupid mother. The woman's name is Tabitha, and she should be considered armed and dangerous. Shoot on sight. Waste the bitch."

Tabitha leaned closer to the officer and lowered her voice so that Rachel could not hear. "Actually, officer, it's my boyfriend. Back at the house, he got angry. He started throwing things. He tried to hit me."

"With a clock?" the patrolman asked.

Tabitha paused for a moment. "Yes. With a clock. I was so scared that I grabbed my little girl and ran."

"Is he the girl's father?"

"No, sir."

"Any reason to think he's following you?"

"I don't think so," Tabitha responded.

"Good girl," the dispatcher said over the patrolman's radio. "Maybe you're not completely useless."

The patrolman nodded. "All right, ma'am. I don't want to hold you up any more, so I'll let you go on two conditions. One, you keep it at seventy even, and not a mile over. Two, you go speak to the police in Dayton tomorrow about a restraining order, because your relationship with your boyfriend is over. Can you do those things for me?"

Tabitha nodded vigorously. "Yes, sir. Absolutely."

"Good." The patrolman stood straight and looked around. Seeing no other cars on the road, he stepped back from the Prius. He pointed his flashlight into the back seat again. "Have a good night, little lady," he said to Rachel. Rachel smiled and waved again. He turned back to Tabitha. "Try not to get too upset while you're driving, okay? Any boyfriend that treats you like that isn't worth the time you spend worrying about him."

"I know," Tabitha said meekly.

The officer turned to leave. Tabitha reached for the gearshift.

"Mommy," Rachel said, looking from the patrolman to Tabitha, "you have a boyfriend?"

Tabitha froze. She spun around to see if the patrolman had heard. He had stopped in the middle of the road. He slowly turned and looked back, his eyes narrowing. He raised his flashlight again and pointed it at Tabitha. Strangely, though, she saw three bright lights: the flashlight and two lights behind it, and they were closing fast.

The tractor-trailer clipped the patrolman from behind, sending him spinning through the air. He cleared the Prius completely, crashed heavily onto the shoulder, and rolled down the roadside embankment. Tabitha watched in horror as his body careened over the car. When she looked back at the road, she saw no sign of any vehicle on the highway, tractor-trailer or otherwise.

"Mommy," Rachel called, "what happened? What was that noise?"

Thank God, Tabitha thought. Rachel didn't actually see it happen. Preoccupied with shock and concern for her daughter, Tabitha slowly opened the driver's door. The moment it unlatched, she heard the whooshing sound of a text message from her phone in the passenger seat. Tabitha instinctively looked at the phone.

Drive. No name. No number. Just the single word.

"Mommy?" Rachel's voice was still calm despite Tabitha's obvious anxiety.

"It's nothing, baby. Just a loud truck."

"Why are you getting out of the car?"

Another whoosh from the phone. *Close the door and drive, Tabitha.*

Tabitha let go of the handle, leaving the door slightly ajar. She stared at the phone, afraid to touch it. Afraid to move.

"Mommy?"

Whoosh. *Don't make me come in there.*

Tabitha opened the door just enough to slam it shut. "I'm not getting out of the car. We're going to Uncle Jason's now, okay? No more interruptions. You go back to sleep."

"But I'm not tired."

"Yes, you are. You'll know you are as soon as you close your eyes."

Rachel narrowed her eyes. "Okay," she said, though the way she drew out the syllables told Tabitha that she didn't believe her.

Tabitha put the car in gear and checked her mirrors to see that the road was still clear. Behind her, she saw the patrol car's lights flashing. She winced and pulled out onto the highway. In the back seat, Rachel tightly squeezed her eyes shut as if to prove her mother wrong. Within minutes, though, the tension eased in her eyelids, and her breathing softened.

Tabitha drove for the next fifty minutes, though she felt as if she spent at least half that time anxiously looking behind her, waiting for the flashing lights of the police who would certainly be coming after her. The road was mostly quiet, though, and she hadn't seen a single cop since she watched one get hit by a phantom truck.

"Apparently," she whispered to herself, "this is my life now."

Tabitha used the dashboard controls to dial Jason's number. The phone rang through the speakers four times before he answered.

"Everything okay, Tabby?"

"Fine," she quickly replied. "I don't know why I said that. Things are horrible."

"Everything will be fine," Jason assured her. "You're probably close, right?"

"We got held up a bit, but we're nearly there. I got onto I-75 a while ago."

"What held you up? Potty break?" His voice was playful, calming.

"No, just...some stuff. I'll tell you later."

"You're not still upset about that cop, are you?"

"What?" she asked, furrowing her brow.

"Forget him." She had called Jason. This voice sounded like Jason. "Did you know he once beat a man almost to death? He's better off broken in a ditch. Or maybe he never existed at all. Maybe you're just going crazy." This was not Jason.

"No."

"Oh yeah, sis. Can't wait for the big family reunion. I'm going to give Rachel a big hug."

Tabitha's eyes narrowed in anger. "You will never touch her."

"Ooo, Tabby's mad." Even the playfulness matched Jason's usual intonations.

"Stop it. Just stop it. Stop sounding like my brother."

"I'm not touching you. I'm not touching you." The voice was still Jason's, but now it sounded like him at ten years old.

"Stop it!"

The speakers crackled, and the radio came on. Some pop song. "I get what I want," the diva wailed. "I get what I want, and I want you!"

The whoosh of a text message. *She belongs to me.*

The radio changed. Hard rock. Growly singer. "You'll never leave this place alive."

The GPS suctioned to the windshield dinged. The subtly mechanical voice of the British woman that Tabitha had found soothing called out: "In half a mile, abandon the car, stand in the middle of the road, and wait for traffic. Then, you have reached your destination."

"Stop it!" Tabitha screamed, pounding her hands against the steering wheel. "Stop it stop it stop it!"

All the noises, voices, and devices went silent.

"Mommy?" Rachel asked groggily from the back seat.

Tabitha took a deep breath. "I'm sorry, baby. Mommy was being too loud."

"Are you mad, Mommy?"

"No, sweetie. Just tired."

"Don't be mad, Mommy," Rachel said matter-of-factly. "It will all be better soon."

"I know. We'll be at Uncle Jason's soon."

"No, Mommy. I mean when I finally take her. Then everything will be better."

Tabitha went numb. Not gradually and not subtly. Completely numb.

"Because she belongs to me," Rachel said calmly. "Rachel is mine."

With trepidation, Tabitha looked in the rearview mirror. Rachel was leaning forward in her car seat, straining against the seatbelt, an eager smile on her face. Tabitha slammed on the brakes so hard that the car banked right before screeching to a stop on the shoulder. She whirled in her seat and locked her gaze with Rachel's sparkling eyes.

"Get out of her," Tabitha hissed.

"We're going to be together forever," Rachel said in a singsong tone. "You will never have her."

"Don't you see how silly you are, Mommy? I'm so much older and more powerful than you are."

"You cannot do this. Be the radio. Be Jason. But get out of my daughter because you cannot have her!"

The GPS dinged. Startled, Tabitha spun to face forward. The radio came to life. NPR, where she had left it. She turned and looked at Rachel; the three-year-old was sleeping peacefully in the back seat.

This...thing...is right, Tabitha thought. "It is older and more powerful than I am, isn't it?" She didn't expect an answer, but one suddenly struck her. "Older and more powerful."

She touched the screen of the GPS to program a new destination. A whoosh from her cellphone. Somehow it knew that she had a plan, that she hadn't broken but intended to resist. She ignored the text. She typed "Maud Hughes Road" into the GPS.

"Getting directions to Hell," the British woman's voice stated. "Make a U-turn when possible—"

"Oh, go fuck yourself," Tabitha said as she ripped the GPS from the windshield and threw it out the window. She opened the glove box and pulled out a map of Ohio. She found Maud Hughes Road just north of Cincinnati. Probably thirty minutes away. Twenty if she floored it.

Another whoosh from her cellphone. Tabitha snatched it up. It joined the GPS.

Tabitha put the car in gear and sped off down the highway.

She had misjudged the distance—or perhaps the speed of her determination—and pulled from the highway toward Maud Hughes Road just fifteen minutes later.

The phone rang through the car speakers despite lying in the road twenty-five miles away. Given everything else, Tabitha wasn't surprised. Without any action from her, the call answered itself.

"Tabby." Jason's voice again. "Where are you going?"

"We're almost there. Wait and see." Tabitha turned the car onto Maud Hughes Road and drove until she reached a high bridge that spanned railroad tracks nearly thirty feet below. She slowed the Prius and parked in the middle of the bridge.

"Decided to end it all here, Tabby?" Jason asked. "It's probably high enough. At the very least, you'll break your legs and be hit by a train before morning."

"Oh, I'm not jumping," Tabitha said.

"No? You're not thinking of throwing Rachel, are you? If you can't have her, no one can?"

"Never. She stays right here with me." Jason's voice was silent, though she could hear that the connection was still open. Tabitha smiled. "You don't know where we are, do you?" More silence. "The Screaming Bridge of Maud Hughes Road." Silence still. "Google it. I did. Growing up haunted, you tend to do a lot of research. I probably know every haunted place in this state."

"Good for you," Jason's voice mocked.

"It's called the Screaming Bridge," Tabitha continued as if it hadn't spoken, "because, according to folklore, a desperate woman threw her baby to its death. She's haunted this place for a very, very long time, screaming and mourning her mistake. She's old, so she's powerful. And ghosts don't get along, right? Given her history, I bet she would really dislike any spirit trying to separate a mother from her child."

"You know nothing."

"I know how to summon her." Tabitha flashed her headlights off and on three times.

"That's ridiculous," the voice growled, barely Jason's now.

"I know, right? I've always wondered who figured out you had to do it three times."

In the darkness just at the edge of the headlights, from the end of the bridge, Tabitha saw something moving toward the car. As it drew closer, she could see that it was a woman dressed in a white robe. As the woman approached, she flickered in and out of existence, each time reappearing about a foot farther. The woman stopped inches from the car and met Tabitha's gaze.

The car started on its own, and the engine revved.

"Please don't let it take my baby," Tabitha whispered at the woman.

The woman reached her hand out and touched the Prius's hood. The car immediately went dead.

The woman flickered and vanished. Tabitha groaned. This had to work. She had been so close. She waited, watching the road. No sign of the woman.

"Hi," Rachel's voice from the back seat.

Tabitha spun around and saw the woman in the back seat, sitting beside Rachel's car seat. Rachel was smiling at her. The woman brushed Rachel's disheveled hair back and smiled at her. She then turned her head, looked at Tabitha, and scowled. The woman flickered again, this time appearing in the passenger's seat. Tabitha watched, hopeful and terrified.

The woman reached forward and touched the tip of her finger to Tabitha's chest. It felt like an icicle. The woman's fingers closed, as if to grasp Tabitha's shirt, but as she drew them away, she pulled something else—a shadow. The shadow stretched as she pulled, clinging to Tabitha. The woman gritted her teeth. With a final tug, she ripped the shadow from Tabitha.

The woman flickered and vanished. Tabitha frantically looked around. She caught sight of the woman outside the car, standing at the rail of the bridge. The shadow in her hands was huge, the size and vague shape of a large man. The woman squeezed it. In response, the shadow swelled, looming over the woman with expanding, misty tendrils flailing out from its mass. As Tabitha watched, the woman pressed on the shadow, struggling to mold it like some mass of translucent clay. Eventually, despite its struggles to resist, she had pressed the shadow into a form small enough to cradle like a child. The woman held it to her breast, rocking it slowly. Then, without warning, she hurled it from the bridge.

The woman looked at the sky and shrieked—a terrible, mournful wail. In mid-scream, she flickered again and vanished.

Tabitha realized she'd been holding her breath. She exhaled and drew clean air into her burning lungs. Her whole body felt lighter, somehow, unrestrained. She looked into the rearview mirror and saw Rachel smiling at her.

"Who was that lady, Mommy?"

"Someone who helped us," Tabitha answered. "Maybe we helped her, too."

"I don't see her anymore," Rachel said, looking around. "Did she go home?"

"I hope so."

"Are we almost at Uncle Jason's?"

"Minor detour, kiddo. We'll be there soon."

THE SUMMER OF GROWING UP

Anne Marie Lutz

The sound of the tires on the road thrummed in Pat's ears. She sat with her head propped on her hand, braced on the car door, and watched miles of fields and trees fly by. Dad had turned off the radio after Captain and Tennille came on for the third time in half an hour, and Mom was reading her new book. Bobby squirmed in boredom, his knobby knees bumping over to Pat's side of the car.

It was the last summer trip she'd ever take with her family. She'd decided that before they left the house.

Bobby's foot slammed into her shin.

"Hey!" Pat snapped. "Stay on your side!"

Bobby stuck out his tongue at her and went back to gazing out the window.

Pat thought she would go crazy. The road lay before them—the same road that she knew from her reading was strewn with fascinating characters and adventure. Her friend Hill had come back from a trip to New York City full of talk of art and actors and weird people on the street playing cool music, wreathed in marijuana smoke. Pat knew that even at home in Ohio, and here in Kentucky, there were people with odd stories, different lives, characters she could draw on when she found the courage to get out of here and head to California.

They had passed into an area close with old trees. The wind whipped through the window and tangled her hair. It was a breath of freedom: the hot humid air, the occasional truck hauling something mysterious, the red car that passed really fast, like her Dad would never drive.

The call of the road pulled at her like a cord tied around her gut, pulling her away from her family.

They pulled into the campground. A man and woman sitting on a blanket in front of an old Scout tent stared at them as the car and trailer parked at the office. Pat leaned her elbow on the car door and stared at the yellow campground sign while Dad went in to register.

Bobby's knees struck her in the thigh. She elbowed him back, hard.

"You two settle down!" Mom said. "We're there, for God's sake."

Bobby whispered at Pat. "That old lady's here again."

Pat looked where Bobby was pointing. The woman who had been at last night's state park was there again, just outside the campground entrance. She sat at her aluminum table, shelling beans into a bowl. A few bright paintings hung on the outside wall of her grayish tent. Inside, Pat saw a row of lumpy figurines on a shelf.

Pat shivered.

"Creepy," Bobby said. "She followed us."

"Shh." Pat opened the door and slid out of the car.

"Pat!" Mom objected. "I don't want you hanging out with those boys at the game room."

"Okay. I'll find you later."

Pat crossed the empty highway to the woman's tent. The road surface radiated heat up through the thin soles of her sandals. The woman smiled at Pat and lifted a hand in greeting. The woman's tight-curled hair seemed almost screwed into her scalp. Pat recognized the flowered dress; it was the same one the woman had worn the day before, at the state park in Ohio.

"Why are you here?" Pat said. It was rude, but Pat felt sort of scared. "Did you follow us?"

"I'm glad to see you again," the woman said. "You're an interesting character. Did your family come to see the wax museum?"

"There's a wax museum?" Pat knew Bobby would whine until they saw it. It was the kind of thing eight-year-old boys liked. "We came to see Mammoth Cave."

"You'll go to the museum, though. Because you like characters too, don't you?" There was a jarring intelligence in the woman's eyes.

Pat nodded. Her eyes traveled to the paintings strung on the side of the tent. They were painted on velvet and tagged with prices in black marker. Further inside the tent was a shelf lined with figurines. They stood in a row, molded in bright colors. There were no price tags on the figures.

"I've gotta go," Pat said. "Parents are waiting."

The woman smiled. "You can call me Hessa. I'll be here tonight if you want to talk."

When Pat found the family's trailer, the outside picnic table had already been covered with newspaper.

"Here, Patty," Mom said. "Set the table." She handed her paper plates and cups. Bobby was near the bathhouse, drawing potable water from the old-fashioned pump.

"Who was that woman?" Mom asked.

"She's selling velvet paintings," Pat said. "I saw her at the park last night."

"In Ohio?" Mom frowned, stopping her sandwich-making. "What's she doing here?"

Pat shrugged.

"Did you say anything about where we were going?"

"No. But she makes wax figures—has a whole shelf of them in there. Maybe she's going to the wax museum."

Mom got a worried look in her eyes. "Your father asked the campground manager about her. He said she shows up now and then, a time or two each summer, camps outside the park entrance on the state verge, and leaves before he can tell her to. Nobody knows who she is."

"It's okay, Mom. I promise I didn't say anything. Do you think we can go to the wax museum?"

"Wax museum!" Bobby crowed. He carried a full pitcher. "I wanna go to the wax museum. That's better than some dumb caves."

§

They stopped at the wax museum after touring the massive caves. Mom wasn't interested; she stayed in the car, parked in the shade of an old tree, reading her Studs Terkel book. The rest of the family wanted to see the famous people the museum brochure had advertised. Pat's legs ached from the day's hiking as they paid and went into the museum.

The rooms were crowded with figures from history, stiff and staring in their costumes. As the family approached each scene a light came on, and a recorded voice told about the wax people who sat behind the Plexiglas.

"Geronimo!" Bobby yelled. The Apache leader wore a red headband that held back his hair. His face was solemn.

"Look, they did one of Jesus," Dad said. Jesus stood looking sort of meditative in his white and red robes. Nearby were figures of Charlie Chaplin and Sammy Davis, Jr.

There were no other tourists there. It made the experience too personal. Pat looked into the almost-real wax faces and thought about being trapped in a room like this, unable to leave.

Her calves ached from the day's climbing at Mammoth Cave. The artificial people stared at her. The air in the museum felt close.

"Can we go?" she asked.

Dad looked around with some distaste. "Yeah, I think we've seen enough. Tourist trap. Come along, Bobby. Let's go to the diner for supper."

The old woman was in her grayish tent by the roadside when they returned to the trailer. After dinner, Pat wandered over to the shed where the campground had a few games. There were two boys playing pinball and smoking, and a girl of about her own age, wearing pink shorts and watching the boys. There was nothing there worth hanging around for.

She waited until two trucks had roared past on the highway and then crossed. The dusk smelled sweet, as if someone had been mowing grass nearby. A few lightning bugs were starting to wink in the weeds. Hessa sat at her table, though it was far too dusky for travelers to see her few velvet paintings for sale. Her hands worked at a lump of something, molding it.

"Come closer," Hessa said. "I don't bite. Did you enjoy the wax museum?"

Pat shrugged. The place had scared her. The people in the exhibits were trapped like bugs under glass.

"Where are you going next?" Hessa asked. She waited a moment, then nodded when Pat did not respond. "That's right. Better not to share with strangers."

Pat looked over her shoulder at her family's trailer in the campground. Dad was sitting at the picnic table. Keeping watch over her, Pat thought.

She twitched her shoulders as if shaking off his protection.

"What's that?" She nodded at the lump of material Hessa was working.

"Just a project," Hessa said. "I need something to keep me busy sitting here all day."

"Do you just travel around, then? Selling your paintings?"

"I go where the road takes me. Isn't that what you want to do?" Hessa's eyes narrowed. Pat felt as if Hessa knew something about her, maybe something Pat didn't even know herself.

And now the old woman was poking into something that didn't concern her. Pat turned away. "Goodbye," she said. "We're leaving tomorrow morning, early. I won't see you again."

"Or you may," Hessa said. "Good night, child."

§

In the middle of the night, with the sound of summer bugs as rhythmic as surf in her ears, Pat decided she'd had enough.

Dad snored in the pullout bed in the front of the trailer. Bobby sprawled on top of his sleeping bag on the floor.

She couldn't stand it any more. She slipped out of her sleeping bag and turned on a flashlight, keeping it shielded under the fabric of her shirt so it wouldn't wake the others. She took her purse and jammed a set of spare underclothes into a bag. She turned the metal handle and opened the door, sliding out into the cool night.

The other trailers and tents were dark. Trees loomed darker than the star-encrusted sky. Pat took a deep breath and headed for the road.

There was no traffic at all. Even though it was the wee hours of the morning, Hessa sat at her table, working something with her hands. A candle flickered in a hurricane lamp, casting shadows.

"I thought so," Hessa said. "You're running away."

Pat couldn't believe the old woman was still sitting there. "What's it matter to you?"

"Nothing, really. Except I told you I like to learn about characters, and you're one. Aren't you? Different from all the others who are afraid to do what you're doing?"

Pat didn't answer. She actually felt rather frightened.

"Is your family so bad?" Hessa's hands kneaded. She was working a lump of something, maybe softened wax. A flickering flame sat under a pan, warming a glob of material on it. The small figurines on the shelf in Hessa's tent writhed and moved with the candlelight. A figure that looked like a farmer, in bib overalls, with a beard and bags under his mournful eyes. A woman's face, round like an apple, with her hair in a bun. A child, smirking at something. Pat hadn't realized before how lifelike the figures were.

"My family's not bad at all," Pat said. She wondered what Mom would feel like when she woke to find her gone. Maybe Pat would find a payphone and a dime and call the campground from the nearest town, just to let them know she was okay. But she couldn't stay. Three more years until high school graduation would kill her; she had to get away.

"Not being abused by anyone? Not running from violence or poverty? Just...a little spoiled?" Hessa asked.

Pat shrugged. It sounded stupid, put like that. Hessa didn't understand the searing desperation to get away, to do something.

"Well, if you must go," Hessa said. Her hands worked, worked.

"That's amazing," Pat said, caught in spite of herself by what Hessa was doing. "I thought wax was too hard to be worked with just your hands."

"This is special wax, my own formulation," Hessa said. "Besides, see? I'm warming it up."

Pat watched the woman's hands almost caress the wax.

"I collect characters," Hessa said. "So if you would tell me about yourself a little before you go, I'd appreciate it."

Pat looked at the wheeling constellations above the treetops, looked at her watch by the light of Hessa's lamp. Two a.m. She could spare half an hour. For some reason she couldn't drag herself away from the old woman with her tight curls, her magical hands, and the row of figures writhing in the candlelight on the shelf.

"What do you mean, you collect characters?"

"I like people," Hessa said. "I collect their stories, if you will. I'd like to hear yours, too. Try to know what you're like. Like that book your mother is reading that tells how people feel about their jobs. Like that."

Mom was reading *Working*, by Studs Terkel. Pat had flipped through the pages. More than just the jobs, it seemed as if people had laid down a bit of themselves in that book.

"Okay. Just for a few minutes."

Hessa put her lump of modeling material on the table. It sat between them, a half-formed lump that could be a blank head, and shoulders like a bust. Or it could be two shapeless blobs.

"Tell me about yourself. Why do you think you need to run away tonight?"

Pat started talking. At first the words came slow, and sounded like she was writing a school paper. Her first name—she didn't trust Hessa enough to give her any more. Her school, with its cliques she did not belong to. What her family did during the summer. How they traveled, stuck in the car with the trailer, and ate Mom's sandwiches and stared out the window at countless fields and barns and little towns.

Then she glanced up at the wheeling stars and realized she would never be here again, and the words spilled out. How she felt stifled, and no one understood. All about the road, even the Tolkien poem she loved about the endless possibilities on the road. About big cities, and dreams. She heard her own voice droning on, talking in a way she never did, telling this woman about herself.

Hessa seemed to fade away, just a shadow across the table.

Pat took a breath and glanced around. The lamp burned lower. The figures on the shelves no longer moved but were just figures again, though they seemed to wait. The lump of wax before her was more detailed than she remembered—surely that was a slope of shoulder, and a fall of long hair.

"There's so much more out there," Pat said. "In California, I can get an acting job, I can do art. I want to paint. I want to be around people who are like me. I heard there are plenty of people out there my age."

The lump on the table looked at Pat. It had eyes, she saw now. Large ones, as long-lashed as her own, with irises of no particular color.

She felt lightheaded. All this emotion had been coiled up inside her for so long. Letting it out—telling Hessa about her deepest dreams, made her almost weak. A chill ran through her, and she leaned hard on the table top.

"Go on," Hessa said. Or had she spoken at all?

"I have big dreams," Pat said. "But everybody's always trying to control me, force me to go to school. There's no one else like me."

Dizziness washed through her. Pat blinked, coming to herself for a brief moment to wonder why she felt so awful now. She leaned on the table. She was perspiring in spite of the cool humid night. Her legs felt rubbery beneath her. She frowned and looked around her. How long had it been since she started talking? And why was the blob of wax on the table looking at her now, with the beginning of high cheekbones, and actual color in the eyes that looked so much like Pat's own?

She pushed back hard from the table. Her chair wobbled. Pat fell, slamming onto her back. She twisted to the side, sprawling in the damp grass. Then she jumped to her feet in spite of the gray haze dropping over her vision.

"Let me help you." Hessa heaved to her feet.

"No!" Pat scrambled for the table and grabbed the wax figure. Her fingers slipped as she swiped it. Something moved under her fingers—an eyelid, twitching—and she yelped as she backed away.

"Come back!" Hessa commanded. "Give it to me."

"It's mine," Pat mumbled. "I know it's mine." She shoved the thing under her shirt, against the warmth of her body. She stumbled away sideways, half-seeing the wax figures on the shelves in the tent, all of them looking at her.

Something wobbled under her foot, and she fell again.

She rolled onto the highway shoulder. Gravel scraped her arms. She clutched the wax figure under her shirt, got to her knees. Something like a hand clutched at her ankle, dragging her back into the grass. She screamed and her voice dropped into the night as if into a well, silenced.

Hessa was behind her, reaching. Pat kicked out hard and felt her shoe strike something soft, maybe Hessa's belly. The woman grunted and let go. Out of the corner of her eye Pat thought she saw the wax figures on the shelf moving, watching.

I collect characters.

She ran then, feet dragging through the grass until she hit the pavement. She ran across the road without looking for traffic, her mind spinning. The thing next to her skin grew soft. She hauled it out when she was near the sole lamppost in the campground. It still had features, but they were blurring, vanishing with Pat's body heat. It was just a lump of wax, and—how had she thought it had eyes? It had no eyes, just little indentations.

The odd fog that had seeped into her mind was clearing. Her legs moved again, swift as she jumped over small obstructions, a fallen deck chair, the ash of an abandoned campfire. A dog howled in the distance, someone's pet perhaps, chained in the yard. It was the first sound other than her own voice and Hessa's voice that Pat had heard for a long time.

She seized the metal handle of the trailer's door and yanked it open, heedless of noise. It swung outward, and Pat's father said, "Who's there?" in a sleepy, alarmed voice.

"It's me," she said, desperate for recognition by someone she loved. "It's Patty."

She looked behind her at the sweep of gray road, grass mounding down to the shoulder. The gray tent was gone, and the old pin-curled woman with it. Within the grasp of her hot hands, all semblance of realism had faded from the lump of wax. She could tell it wasn't...whoever it had been trying to become.

The blood thrummed in her veins; fear shook her hands. Her mind was clear and she knew exactly who she was. She flung herself into her Dad's arms.

Mom sat up next to Dad, her voice worried. "Patty, what's wrong?"

"I'm back," Pat said. "I want to go home. Right now."

"There, there," Dad said.

Bobby still slept sprawled in his sleeping bag, unaware of the commotion. Pat felt vaguely comforted by this—all as it should be, with her family around her.

She glanced out the trailer door before pulling it shut behind her. The road beckoned, a thin silver strip leading away from the campground. It pulled at her heart. But her family, shuffling around in the cramped trailer trying to comfort her, pulled too. Mom started warming some milk to help Pat get back to sleep.

The road would still be there next summer.

BILLY WHITE'S DOG

Emily Hitchcock

He had been walking for a long time. Pitch bubbled up from cracks in the highway and sweat trickled down the back of his neck. The road was still. Semis had turned to pickup trucks after he headed off the freeway toward Piedmont. Traffic tapered off with each mile, and instead of sticking to the cover of the woods, he walked boldly on the other side of the guardrail.

The sun reddened.

He figured his chances of getting picked up before nightfall were slim. He looked over his shoulder at the shimmering empty road and surveyed himself critically. Dust stuck to sweat stuck to yesterday's grime. Dirt-colored, lank hair hung raggedly to the bottom of his jawline. A patchy beard spread down his face and neck, almost meeting his chest at the collar of a dirty T-shirt.

He cinched up the piece of nylon rope holding up his jeans. The last trucker had eyed his skinny frame and demanded he turn his arms, wrists up.

Shit. What I can smell of myself must be only half as bad as what I've already gotten used to.

He walked on.

Faintly he heard the white-noise whoosh of air moving past a vehicle. He slowed his steady trudge, feeling the blacktop tremor slightly through thin soles.

Feels too big to be a trooper or a local cop—unless it's a K-9.

He hesitated, eyeing the cover beyond the guardrail. Vagrancy laws varied widely. Some cops were nice enough, most weren't.

He was too tired not to try. He turned to face the oncoming vehicle, thumb out.

Expressions are tricky. Give 'em your best I'm-not-a-serial-killer-smile? Shiiiit. I probably look like Charles Manson.

He kept his face impassive as a dark-colored SUV came into sight. It was the first vehicle he'd seen for at least a mile. The driver braked, the SUV's tires popping gravel, hazard lights blinking. He caught sight of himself in the reflection of the tinted passenger window just before it lowered.

Yep. Young Charles Manson.

He tried to make his eyes friendlier.

A pretty, dark-haired, round-faced woman leaned toward the open window. Her eyes passed over his pointy elbows, his loose posture, his pained expression. Her expression was kind. The passenger seat was empty.

"Well hullo there. Where ya headed?" she chirped through thick lips.

"Piedmont."

His mouth was filled with dust he hadn't noticed before. He drew up some spit from the back of his throat and hocked it out onto the road. A string of spittle dangled from his lip. He looked up at the woman and quickly added, "Ma'am."

"Well then. Looks like we're all headed in the same direction. Hop in if you'd like a lift."

All? Boyfriend/husband/dad must be in the back seat, probably pissed off and mean.

He tried to get a look through the back window but the tint was too dark. Air conditioning and air freshener wafted over him from the open window. The woman's teeth were extra white. The power locks were already up.

The woman smiled as he popped open the passenger door. He slung his backpack onto the floor and turned to check the back seat as he hoisted himself into the SUV. The back of the vehicle was filled with luggage. The back seat was occupied by a toddler.

A kid? A godamned kid.

His mind flicked through all the sick people he'd met during his time on the road. He could be any one of them.

"My name is Alice and that's Mary-Anne," the woman said.

The curly-haired little girl narrowed watery brown eyes. She snatched up a neon pink monkey from the seat next to her and shoved it down the side of her car seat.

He turned around slowly, lowering himself in his seat. The woman was looking expectantly, patiently at him.

"Oh… Charles," he lied.

"Nice to meet you, O' Charles," she said. Her laughter was girlish. "Seatbelt on, please."

The woman waited for him to click his seatbelt into place before she put on her blinker and merged back onto the empty highway.

He watched her watch the road from his peripherals, noticing how she kept two hands on the wheel. The e-brake was between them—push button down, then lift up. The windows were automatic, the locks were too.

He leaned his arm casually on the window switch. The window cracked open. He eyed the glove compartment.

"What brings you way out here on your own?" the woman said.

He used the conversation as an excuse to sneak a look at her. Her dark hair was pulled into a thick ponytail. Sleek black dress pants bulged with residual baby fat. Beige silk, unstained despite the presence of a toddler, clung in revealing ripples, even as she self-consciously tried to pluck it away from herself. Diamond studs, thin gold tennis bracelet, no wedding ring.

Big tits, perky smile, perky smell, perky fucking voice. Damn. If only more truckers on the road were more like Alice.

"I got a brother in Piedmont," he rasped, lying again. "Just trying to catch a break in another town." He'd noticed people seemed more comfortable if you had a destination. It wasn't entirely a lie. His brother just didn't know he was coming. Yet.

"I have a brother about your age. Backpacked around the country with a friend a couple years ago before he settled on a college. Do your folks know you're out here? I bet they worry."

She looked at him expectantly from her peripherals. He looked straight ahead.

"Uh huh."

She fidgeted. Uncomfortable. Grinding the conversation forward, the woman began to chatter, picking up momentum as she talked, filling in the gaps of his sparse explanations with her own.

"Anyway, we're on our way up north for a visit." She glanced back in the rearview mirror at the girl. "Mary-Anne and I have been keeping each other company for the past two days." The girl stayed quiet in the back seat. "She's not much of a talker either."

He let her tell him about their trip, about Fourth of July fireworks they'd seen and truck stop dinners. She rambled on, looking sideways at him sometimes, but mostly keeping her eyes on the empty road. He could hear the smile in her voice.

He gave her a nod now and then, and that was enough to keep her going, her sticky lipglossed lips continuously moving, the makeup line around her second chin disappearing and reappearing. He watched her watch the road, and stared at her openly when he was sure she was distracted. His heart began to beat a little faster.

She drove with both hands on the wheel, chubby hands and stubby fingers leading into thick wrists and soft arms. He'd known a kid with hands like that.

Fat Billy White, always following us around, trying to be friendly... Damned if I wasn't already an asshole at eight years old.

He smiled at the recollection of his younger self, dry lips cracking a little in the climate controlled air of the present, crooked yellow teeth showing for a moment. The woman caught his change of expression and smiled along with whatever story she was telling. Encouraged now, she continued to talk. Her breasts strained against her silk blouse with every inhale, taking out a little more seatbelt slack.

Billy's sister had tits and so did Billy. We didn't want him around, but we sure did want his sister. A bunch of us threw a glass of water on her and ran away, didn't even have the guts to see her nipples like we'd planned.

He gave the woman another "Uh huh" to keep her going before settling back in his seat and letting his eyes drift out of focus.

Rounding the corner on Billy White, watching as he stuck out his little, chubby hand and that dog, not his dog any more, looked wild at him before he lunged.

Billy still didn't see it coming.

He looked at the woman.

"You can adjust the radio if you want."

He looked at the smooth, shiny buttons glowing cool electric blue in the darkening car. He looked at the dials and the AUX ports and the iPod jack and the LED faceplate.

Two hundred dollars. Two-fifty at the right shop.

"I wouldn't know how to work that thing."

The woman reached over, pressed a button and "Wheels on the Bus" began to play. The little girl in the back began to sing, warbling along a beat behind the track. The woman hummed along, tapping chubby fingers on the steering wheel. The trees had turned to fields that spread out on either side of the road in the twilight.

He thought about all the times he'd had to come up with ways to take control in a vehicle barreling down the highway.

A little tap to the steering wheel is all it'd take. Off the road, out of sight.

The woman hummed on. They passed a gas station billboard.

A throat chop, a sucker punch, an elbow to the stomach, a gouge in the eyeballs. Plus the kid. You could do anything to the kid in a situation like this.

He looked at the woman again. She looked happy. He continued to watch her as he bent down and opened his backpack. He jerked the zipper hard, purposefully, and it unzipped audibly. The woman glanced over once, but her eyes went back to the road.

Nothing.

He rummaged around with one hand, watching the woman. He started to sweat.

Ask me what I'm doing. Slow down. Reach for your cellphone. Tense up. Look nervous.

"I'm going to stop at this gas station up the road if that's okay with you," the woman said.

There it is. Fear.

"I'm pretty sure Mary-Anne needs to be changed and I could use a bathroom break myself."

The smell of shit hit him. It wasn't an excuse.

"That'd be fine, ma'am," he said, eyes on her, hand in his backpack. "I'd better be going my separate way after this stop, anyway."

His hand closed on something cold, something sharp. He thought about the time a trucker pulled a Bowie on him. He'd pissed himself.

This must've been what that trucker bastard felt like, having complete power over another person, knowing he had me.

He started to breathe heavier, the air conditioning drying his mouth with every inhale.

"Well if you're sure. I'm glad we could at least get you a little farther down the road." The woman looked back at the child again and smiled over at him. "Guess it's just you and me again, Mary-Anne." The little girl had fallen asleep.

The SUV slowed, and the woman clicked on the turn signal early, pulling into the little gas station and stopping at the last pump. It was the sort of off-highway place that cars passed by in favor of bigger truck stops. The electric lights buzzed audibly, casting everything in a harsh, greenish glow. The woman's SUV was the only vehicle on the lot. He could see the gas station attendant stocking cigarettes inside, back turned to the smeared Plexiglas.

He unbuckled his seatbelt and turned slowly in his seat. The woman was rummaging around in her purse, eyes down. He lifted his hand slowly from within the backpack, the once-cold metal warmed now by his clenched hand.

The woman put down her purse and looked up at him suddenly with her soft, round face. He froze, hand half in, half out of his bag.

"Here. Take this and buy yourself a bus ticket, or at the very least, a good dinner. And don't try to argue. And call your parents, or your sister if you've got one." She winked at him.

He stared at the woman's outstretched hand, her small chubby fingers so close to him now. For the first time that evening, before he closed the distance between them, he looked her right in the eyes. She never saw it coming.

The woman was still smiling as he slid the little blade into her soft belly. Her eyes were still focused on him as he slid the knife back out and in again. She yelped as a splotch of red bloomed on her pretty silk shirt and she reached down, clutching at his hand, but not screaming, just staring, her lips parted in a surprised, "Oh."

The woman's face slowly lost color under her makeup, the skin between her eyes pinched together in confusion, her outstretched hand falling limply to the seat, letting go of the twenty dollars.

"But I…"

He looked at the woman's kind face, her honest surprise. Watching her carefully, keeping her pinned with the knife, he reached up with his other hand and adjusted the rearview mirror to reflect the sleeping child in the back seat. And this time, finally, he saw real fear. He reached over and turned up the stereo as the woman began to scream.

It was fully dark as he walked away from the SUV, quickly crossing the perimeter of light around the gas station. He headed back to the highway shoulder, warm knife in one hand, folded neatly into his palm, crumpled twenty-dollar bill in the other.

As he walked, he thought about how far he had yet to go, but mostly, he thought about Billy White's dog.

RENDEZVOUS IN GRASS VALLEY

Wayne Rapp

In the spring of 1976, my daddy turned mean. Mama said it was because of the strike talk at the mines, but I was pretty sure it was something else. Like his girlfriend leaving town with her husband to move to Grass Valley. I was fourteen that year, a gangly, pimple-faced reminder of my daddy's parental obligations, the anchor that held him from picking up and following her.

I loved Mama, but God, it galled me that she was so out of it. Or maybe she just pretended not to notice what everyone else in San Pedro, Arizona knew. My shortcut home from school took me right past Doreen Lathrop's house, and after seeing my daddy's pickup parked along her side yard a couple of times, I couldn't stand it any more. I started taking the long way home. Evidently that's what Daddy was doing too. Doreen's husband worked second shift in the mines, a convenience that allowed the truck to be parked next to her house for hours. Mama thought Daddy stopped off for a few beers a lot more often than he used to and made comments to that effect. Daddy coming home half on his ass with beer on his breath most nights seemed only to solidify her thinking.

On some of these nights, Daddy could be easy-going and happy. Sometimes, though, he was moody, and I learned to stay away from him. After Doreen Lathrop left town, he was angry all the time, and, as his son living in the same house, there was no way I could get away from his meanness. He tore into me for the least little thing. He didn't like the way I combed my hair or ate my dinner. He threatened to kick my ass out of the house almost every night. Mama would get in the middle of it then and calm him down. I looked at her sad face and knew it was best for me not to push it with him. We lived in a small wood-frame house like most in our hardscrabble mining town, and when Daddy started stomping around, there was no place to escape his wrath. Instead, I would retreat to the hill behind our house to get away from him.

Things were rough for me that spring, and the miners continued to talk strike. Daddy would rail on and on about the company and how they were screwing the miners. He talked tough about how the men needed to stand up to the company. Not let themselves be pushed around. Mama, in her non-confrontational way, did not counter his rants, but more than once while I was helping her with the dishes she said that when push came to shove, he would be like all the rest. I asked her once what she meant.

"It happens every time," she said. "You wait and see. The company will start increasing the men's overtime and bonus rates. The men will think they have to take all the overtime they can handle so they can save some money in case they go out on strike. But they never figure it's a trap."

She stood at the sink, sweat on her face and a strand of hair hanging in her eyes, her hands moving in an easy rhythm, talking as she washed. "If they do go out, the company will have a huge surplus of copper that came from the bonuses and overtime, and they'll be able to hold out that much longer. That extra money the miners make won't last half as long as that extra copper, plus the price of copper will go up to boot."

Mama was right, but along with offering the bonuses and overtime, the company began a few layoffs, sending the message that those who didn't appreciate their jobs or understand management's position might be sent packing at any moment. Doreen Lathrop's husband had been one of those unfortunates. The word was that he had a cousin in Grass Valley, California, and had decided to head west and north from San Pedro to try to get a job in the gold mines.

Others from our town had gone before him during the rough times of past years, so that there was a small colony of San Pedro miners already living there.

During one of Daddy's nightly rants at my mother, out of the blue, he started talking about going to Grass Valley. "Tired of all this shit in San Pedro. Ready to walk away and start over."

Daddy had a lot of energy and was always moving. Seldom did he sit still. He was small and wiry and tended to strut around instead of walking. "Like a banty rooster in a packed hen house," Mama's brother Jim, who didn't much like Daddy, used to say.

"You can't quit your job, Clel. You've got sixteen years in."

"And it can all be over tomorrow if the company wants it to. When you start closin' in on your twenty, the company just looks for things to keep you off that retirement list."

"Well, don't they do that all over?" my mama asked. "What company wants to pay out money to men who aren't working for them any more?"

"Banner Mines doesn't do that up in Grass Valley. Least that's the way I hear it."

"Now who do you know in Grass Valley?" Mama asked innocently.

"I know lots of people in Grass Valley, Ida," Daddy said. "They call back to San Pedro; they keep in touch with their families and friends."

Yeah, I know just who Daddy's talking about. Recklessly, I intruded into the tense air that was forming around the kitchen table, hanging there like mid-day heat. "How do you know for sure there's going to be a strike?"

"Who the hell asked you into this conversation?" Daddy fired back. "I'm talking to your mother."

"Nobody," I answered meekly. "I just don't want to move away. I don't want to leave my school."

"Oh yeah, 'cause all those girls that hang all over you wouldn't know what to do if you weren't around," my daddy said cruelly, knowing full well that my skin condition and self-conscious personality kept me in the background.

"I just don't want to move," I said, recognizing my daddy's building anger and starting to back out of the room.

"You aren't part of this," he said, voice rising. "Get the hell out of here."

I moved quickly, not wanting to incur any more of his wrath. I stayed close by, though, listening to the one-sided conversation from the next room, as my daddy kept pounding home his point about getting out of San Pedro and starting over. Not letting the company run his life. *Doreen Lathrop must have set a deadline for him.*

As school ended for the year and summer began, Daddy's appeal to my mother to leave for Grass Valley became more intense. It all came to a head late one afternoon as we sat around the table after supper while Daddy smoked a cigarette. "We wait around 'til the strike starts, and there won't be any jobs left in Grass Valley," Daddy reasoned. "Miners from here will be all over the place in a few days, and it'll be too late."

"What kind of mining do they do up there?" Mama asked.

"Gold mining. Copper here, gold there. All hard rock mining. Break my back up there as well as here."

"How do you even know there are jobs there now?" Mama said.

"Damnit, Ida. We been over this before. I hear from people in Grass Valley that Banner Mines is hiring. I know, so quit badgering me about it."

"I'm sorry, Clel. I just don't see you quitting your job and taking the risk."

Daddy sprung his trap. "I know you've never liked San Pedro all that much. Bein' so dry and all. That's why a change might be good for all of us. I think you'd like living somewhere with some green. Remind you a little more of Kentucky. I want to take a week of my vacation and go up there and check it out."

"I thought you were going to save that vacation in case you went out on strike?"

"I'd still have two weeks left. Besides, if we leave, we won't have to worry about the strike."

He had her, and my mother knew it. "If you go, why don't you take Donnie with you? He's out of school, and it'll give him a chance to see some of the country."

"No," I blurted. "I don't want to go." But both of my parents ignored me.

"And what am I supposed to do with him while I'm out looking for work?" Daddy was clenching and unclenching his fists as if he wanted to hit somebody.

"Donnie's a big boy. He can stay in a motel room by himself and read or something."

Daddy glared hard at me, his face beginning to flush.

He must have had other plans for that motel room.

I had to get out of there. I fled to the hill behind our house and began to climb—past the scrub oak and cholla, the century plants and mesquite—

until I reached a trail that ran diagonally up across the face of the hill. I was loping, getting away from the house as quickly as I could. As I climbed, the town came into view, and past it, the dark gallows frames that guarded the underground copper shafts. This was the scene I loved—the town and its industry nestled among the hills and canyons. People living and working close together, giving San Pedro its unique character, a color all its own. I didn't know how I could bear to leave it.

When I returned home an hour later, the plan had been set. Mama had somehow prevailed. "Looks like you and me are goin' travelin'," Daddy sneered, as I squeezed sideways past him on the way to my bedroom. "We're gonna leave Saturday when I get off shift and drive all night, and if you're not ready, I won't wait an extra minute." It was a threat. He was looking for any reason to leave me behind, and I thought that might be my way out. Go somewhere. Not be home when he was ready to leave.

Mama came to my bedroom later that evening, something she hadn't done since I was in grade school. I was lying on my bed with clothes on, my right forearm covering my eyes. She sat down next to me and took my hand, pulling my arm away from my face, the harsh light from the bulb in the hallway illuminating the room and making me squint to look up at her sadness.

"Donnie, don't be mad at me, please. I can't turn him loose to go up there alone, and I can't face that woman. I just don't know what I'd do if I ever had to look at her knowing she was trying to steal your daddy." She got up and left as quietly as she'd come. I lay there for a minute before I sat up. So Mama did know after all. She just didn't know what to do about it. And if she didn't, what was I supposed to do? Whatever it was, I knew I couldn't let her down.

Mama had dinner ready to put on the table when Daddy walked in from his shift that Saturday. She also had his clothes packed in our only suitcase and mine folded neatly in a paperbag. "You're going to have to look through and pick out your shaving things, Clel. I don't know that much about it." The sadness in her face made me want to cry, and I had to turn away.

Daddy went to get his shaving gear together, and Mama started putting the food on the table, and while Daddy and I ate, she busied herself packing lunches for the next day. I was normally a fast eater—one of the things Daddy frequently got on me about—but this afternoon I couldn't keep up with him. He was shoveling it in. "Hurry up," he said to me. "As soon as I go to the bathroom and put stuff in the truck, I'll be ready to go. I want to get on the road."

Mama stood behind me and rubbed my shoulders as I quickly finished my dinner. "There's an extra piece of cake in your lunch sack that he don't need to know about if you're careful," she whispered.

When the truck was loaded, Daddy surprised me. He took hold of Mama and gave her a kiss. "Be seein' you soon," he said, as he patted her on the bottom. Mama left his arms and gave me a big hug. The side of my face was wet with her tears as she pulled away. I watched her lift her hand in a half-hearted wave as we backed out of the driveway.

I stared out the window as the pickup climbed out of the canyon and crested the scrub oak and juniper-covered hills. When we came down the other side and crossed the near-dry river, I knew my beloved town was behind me. Only the long, empty road lay ahead. Neither my daddy nor I said anything for forty miles. He spent most of the time fiddling with the radio, trying to hold it on a country station that kept drifting in and out of range. "Wish you were old enough to drive," he grumbled. "This is a hell of a long trip for one man to drive straight through."

Should have thought about that when you told Doreen Lathrop you were coming.

By midnight, we were still in Arizona, and I had no idea how much of California we would have to travel to reach Grass Valley. We stopped once for gas and to stretch our legs. Daddy bought a cup of coffee. Said he needed it to keep him awake. He offered to buy me a Coke, but I refused, figuring sleeping was the easiest way for me to get through this trip. I didn't want to sit up all night and watch the road's mile markers carry me farther away from my home.

Some time during the night, I was aware of my daddy pulling the truck off the road. He rolled his jacket up into a pillow and leaned it against the window. "Can't do no more," he said as he dropped off to sleep. I don't know how long he was down, but the next thing I knew we were on the road again, and daylight was chasing us.

We drove west, following signs toward Los Angeles. I brightened a bit and wondered if we'd see the ocean before the day was over, but then we turned north toward Sacramento and began to climb, and I hoped our three-year-old Ford pickup was up to the long haul. We stopped for gas and for Daddy's coffee and cigarettes. "Some fruit in your bag if you're looking for breakfast," he said to me. I had been nibbling cake every chance I got until I'd eaten the extra piece Mama had given me. I was okay.

Daddy looked absolutely worn out. "Just talked to the fellow inside the station," he said, throwing a California map on the seat between us. "We aren't but a little over halfway. Didn't know it was so damn far."

Guess Doreen Lathrop must have forgot to tell you that. I pulled a peach out of my bag and buried the wax paper from my extra piece of cake. Before I started in on the peach, I unfolded the map and tried to find out where we were. Daddy was right; we still had a long way to go to reach Grass Valley.

The roads were wider and better maintained in California than in Arizona, so the driving didn't seem as hard. Course I was just riding. Daddy was the one fighting with the big trucks and the mountains. I wasn't used to looking at all the green of the valleys and mountains around me. It was pretty, but right then I would have traded it easily for the brown hills and canyons that were home to me.

On one occasion, Daddy seemed glad that I was studying the map. I kept him from following a direction that would have made our trip longer. He didn't believe me at first, even pulled off the road to check the map himself, but finally he followed my route. Even with my little shortcut, our trip turned out to be just over a thousand and fifty miles and took us almost twenty-three hours. It was going on five p.m. Sunday when we drove up to the first motel we came to in Grass Valley. It didn't take long to register and get our things inside.

I could tell Daddy was exhausted, his eyes red and droopy from lack of sleep, but there was a little smile on his face as he strutted to the motel room door. "I'm going out for a bit," Daddy said. "I've got to call some people and let them know I'm in town. Find out where the mine employment office is for tomorrow. We'll get something to eat when I get back."

I looked at the phone sitting next to the bed but didn't ask the obvious question.

I had never been in a motel room before and didn't know what to expect. This one sure wasn't much. There was a TV with rabbit ears on a metal stand, a double bed, small dresser and a nightstand with a lamp. Looks like Daddy and me were going to have to sleep together. An open door led to a small bathroom.

When I couldn't get anything to come in on the TV set, I lay down and quickly went to sleep. Daddy pounding on the door an hour later woke me up. He had a sack of hamburgers in his hand, and he didn't look all that happy.

Now that I was awake, I was starved. Sitting on the end of the bed with Daddy, I gulped down two hamburgers with some water from the bathroom faucet. There were french fries, too, but I worked on them carefully. There was only one sack of fries, and I wasn't sure whether I was meant to share them with Daddy or not. He was silent, munching slowly on a hamburger. I didn't want to ask him about the fries, so I passed them to him. He took them but sat them down between us, not touching them. I eyed them greedily but decided to let them sit. Daddy finally finished one burger and started on a second. After a couple of bites, he stopped eating. "You want the rest of this?" he asked. I took it from his hand and pulled the fries over next to me while Daddy stared into space. I didn't know if he was just tired, but there was an obvious slump to his shoulders. I finished eating in a couple of minutes and wadded up my wrappings and put them back into the sack. "Take that outside and throw it into the garbage can over by the office," Daddy ordered. "I don't want any bugs sleeping in here with us."

The hamburger sack was in the garbage can, and I was putting the lid on when I heard the noise. I turned to see a very big man pounding on the door to our motel room. "Come on out here, Sanders. You and me need to talk."

I stood there frozen, watching as Daddy opened the door. "Now, Art," he said, and that's all he got out of his mouth before the big man punched him in the face, sending Daddy hurtling back through the open door. The man pushed right into the room after him.

I went flying across the parking lot to our room and could see the man continuing to punch my daddy, who was sprawled across the bed trying to cover up and protect himself. I landed square on the man's back, trying with all my might to pull him away. The man's big arm swept around and sent me sprawling into the wall, where I slipped silently to the floor in a daze.

From where I lay, I could see my daddy push hard against the man to get him off his body. "Godamnit, Art. That's my son. Leave him alone." Daddy freed himself and knelt next to me, lifting me gently to my feet, his eyes scanning me for injury.

"Your son?" the man fumed. "What was he supposed to do? Be your lookout? Watch out for me while you were screwing my wife?"

I'd never seen him before, but I knew the man who'd just pounded my daddy had to be Doreen Lathrop's husband. He stood, breathing hard, in bell-bottom sailor pants with his blue work shirt unbuttoned about halfway down, displaying a thatch of dark chest hair. His fists were still clenched.

My daddy kept his arm around my shoulder, a sheepish look on his face. "He's got no part in this. Never has. Just traveling with me while I look for work."

"You get laid off, too?"

"Not yet, but I wasn't aimin' to wait around for it."

"So you just happened to pick Grass Valley as a place to come? Followed my wife up here, even though one of our reasons for coming was so she could get away from you?"

Daddy's face grew sullen. "That ain't true."

"Oh, yeah? What did she tell you tonight?"

I knew something had happened earlier that hadn't set well with Daddy. He had that same unhappy look on his face that he had when he came back to the motel an hour ago.

"How do you think I knew where to find you?"

When Daddy didn't answer, Mr. Lathrop moved to the door, then stopped, clenched his fists and came back.

He stood looking at my daddy, shook his head and then slowly unclenched his fists. "I don't figure you, Clel. You got a wife who's not running around on you. You got a boy that jumped in the middle of a fight to save your ass, not thinkin' he might get hurt. You got a job. You got seniority and good time toward a pension. I got none of those. If I did, I'd get in that pickup out front and drive as fast as I could back to San Pedro. What the hell is it with you?"

Daddy dropped his head and wouldn't answer.

Mr. Lathrop stood there for a few seconds staring at Daddy then turned and walked out of the room. Daddy rushed to the door and locked it then came quickly back to me. "Are you okay?" he asked.

I was looking at the welt that was growing across Daddy's cheek and knew he was hurt a lot worse than I was. "I'm all right," I assured him.

He looked at me for a minute with such a sad expression that I was afraid he might start to cry. He sat down then on the end of the bed and covered his face with his hands. I didn't know what to say. I could only sit and stare at him. After a while, he got up and headed into the bathroom. "Better get ready for bed," he mumbled to me on his way.

I didn't realize how tired I really was until my head hit the pillow. I slept peacefully the whole night. I wasn't ready to get up when Daddy shook me before daylight. "Come on. I've already checked out. We've got to get an early start." I dressed while Daddy loaded our things into the truck, and then we were on the road. My sense of direction told me we were driving south, every mile taking us farther away from Grass Valley.

We drove until the sun came up, and then Daddy stopped and bought me a big breakfast at a truck stop. While I was finishing eating, he excused himself and went to the phone booth in the back of the diner. I watched as he talked into the phone. I assumed he was talking to Doreen Lathrop. He returned with a hint of his familiar strut, and despite the angry welt that still covered one cheek and an eye that was dark and swollen, he had a bit of a smile on his face. I thought we might be turning around and heading back to Grass Valley, but after he paid the bill, we were back on the road heading south.

"That was your mama I was talking to. She was glad to hear we were on our way home. Said to say hello and tell you she'd make a meatloaf for you when you got home. I told her that would taste good for both of us."

We drove in silence for a few miles. From time to time I would glance in Daddy's direction. He didn't look like the angry, mean man I'd seen for the last couple of months. I could tell he was having trouble seeing out of his swollen eye, and as I watched, the eye began to tear. Daddy blinked and shook his head in short, sorrowful arcs, and then he pulled the truck off on the side of the road, put it in neutral, and set the emergency brake. Quickly he opened his door and got out. In the rearview mirror I saw him pass the back end of the truck and disappear. I sat in my seat and listened to the engine idle. It didn't drown out the sound of Daddy throwing up.

I waited a minute, expecting him to get back into the truck, and when he didn't, I got out. I found Daddy sitting on his back bumper, his head hung low, cradled in his hands. I stood there not knowing what to say.

After a few seconds, he lifted his head and looked at me. "Donnie," he said, with tears in his eyes, "I am so sorry and ashamed. I'll never forget how it felt to have my son see something like that."

Daddy was struggling with what he had to say, but I could tell he was determined to get through it. "This story won't all come out in one telling. Not the whole of it. It'll take some time for me to work it out with your mama. She needs to see the shame in me that you saw last night, and I don't expect you to be able to forgive me just yet, either. But we got time to work it out between us if you will."

There was a choke in my throat. I couldn't talk. I just nodded.

"Now let's get on the road," Daddy said, and when we got back into the truck, he smiled and passed me the map. "Find us a quick way home, son. You know how to read this map better'n me."

Shadow of the Spider

Alice G. Otto

The eggs ooze. The scrambled mounds leak liquid like wounds spitting puss. The toast is gauze, soaking up the mucus mess of runny chicken potential. The plate glares white at the edges. Everything soft and wet and crisp and dry merges there, collides there, a wreck of sickly yellow.

And in the pepper spattered across this flaxen landscape, I see Florida. Snaking about and around the Gulf. Stretching between lips of moist salt. Florida. Tossing its curious keys forward and stirring lizards with lightning.

I blink to find black and gray specks. A random pattern of spice. The gulls stop crying that quickly. Something close to silence, and I will not eat these eggs.

They are perfect. Undercooked, untouched, and perfect—too much so to eat.

I nudge the plate aside. The waitress humors my request to pour my orange juice into a coffee mug rather than a glass. I pour creamer into the mug, and only the waitress sees through the illusion. The rims of her eyes tense.

"Orange cream," I say. She is not convinced. "Orange and cream, good pair. Yogurt. Candies," I pause for a full swallow, "ice cream." I add another shot of cream. "Guess it'd look funny, doing this to juice, but if people think it's coffee, then nothing's funny. That's all it is, a trick, an illusion. Who knows, right, maybe it's actually coffee."

"Yeah…if you need anything else, holler. Here's your bill, have a good morning." The waitress retreats to the greasy counter.

The eggs lie still now, stagnating in a pool of their own juices. I picture a miniature waitress drowning there. If not for the map, I would forget where I am. Coast to coast, the servers are all the same, early shifts in highway diners. Nebraskan blotched skin and Pennsylvanian morning mascara and Californian teased hair melt into a ubiquitous portrait of Americana, dusty and archetypal. The nicotine-driven welfare woman peddling hot refreshments from a tray perched atop a permanently craned wrist. I want to fill a vat with weeping scrambled eggs and invite them all to jump in. They would shed their stained aprons, sink deeper and deeper without struggle, until the lumpy mess consumed them. And somewhere down the line, their thank-you letters, penned for me alone, would emerge from the yellow depths in envelopes sealed with sticky yolk.

It is time to leave. I had chosen the table of three truckers, by the exit, but the family of four appears to be finished as well, a couple of booths away. Relying on one table is risky, but two almost always pans out. The seventh and final customer clears the doorway. I tuck the unpaid bill beneath my untouched plate of food and rise. The nausea of hunger and exhaustion peaks and regresses with the sensation of legs pumping a swing into motion. My gut launches hot fireworks to the base of my skull. Sparks pierce my brain.

My translucent reflection in the glass door approaches, a murky skeleton. Tufts of crinkled black hair throw the concave cheeks into deeper shadow. Knobby hipbones protrude over cargo pants, cinched in place by a length of thin red rope. The muscles allowing this figure to move must hide, compacting tight, to let the skin clutch as close to bone as it does. This is not me. I continue walking toward the reflection, and when my left hand darts to the first dirty booth, the mirrored figure's hand closes around several bills and stuffs them in her pocket. Closer now, my eyes are wide and dark and moist, there. I snatch the tip from the truckers' table. Her mouth is flaking and pale. I clamp my lips between my teeth, reach forward, our hands meet against the glass, finger to finger and thumb to thumb. I push myself away. As the door swings open, she disappears in glinting slivers. The warm dust of the parking lot coats my lungs. I stride to my car, key already in hand. Some flicks of the wrist, flex of the foot, and I am gone.

§

Back on the highway, I pick the dollars out of my pocket and drop them on the passenger side of the bench seat: one, two, three, four, five. I switch lanes to pass a crawling semi. Five, six, seven, eight. Eight dollars, eight slips of faded green paper, a few more gallons of gasoline. The truckers most likely accounted for six, two apiece, being generous in their affinity with the worn waitresses along their routes. The quaint family, two, probably vacationers who only stopped at the diner because the next McDonald's was twenty miles out. No appreciation for the flavor of those places. The sad timelessness and universality.

"But they paid their bill," I say, "and money's what matters, money is matter and the value of orange cream."

I drive for several more hours. If a sign says south, I follow it. Daylight dwindles, and my hands take on the appearance of five-legged pasty spiders grasping the steering wheel. It used to scare me how daddy-long-legs could extend and contract their fibrous limbs. I wondered where they hid the power in their skinny frames. I watch my index finger stretch to turn off the air conditioning. I close and open the joints, mesmerized. Disturbed. I need to eat. I rub my arm with my opposite hand, following it to the shoulder, down the ribcage, to my midriff. My hand is not a spider, it is definitely attached to my body. Perhaps my body is a spider.

My car glides into a rest area exit lane. Not a conscious decision, but it never is. I cut the engine. How many times have I looked out on this exact scene, the brick restrooms and shelves of tourist brochures and tidy bundles of vending machines? The texture of the earth and the state names proudly printed on the glossy pamphlets change. The mutilated carcasses thrashed about the pavement's yellow and white lines change. No armadillos here, raccoons there, a wild turkey, farther north. I allow warm water to drain from the corner of my eye. I visualize the hot sparks flowing out of my brain to the bench seat below, flames laying claim to the tan upholstery, embracing my empty head with warmth.

I slap the glove box and it falls open. The rummaging arachnid at the end of my arm produces the tired map. The map, laced in straight pins, unfolds with more difficulty each time. The points catch upon one another and the paper. It is a snare and a lost cause. Somehow the picture is intact. A topographical rendering, illustrating the highs and the lows of the United States. I began in the thin air, elevated, but unaware of that. Colorado. That first pin has a little red head, and tiny blooms of rust. My fingers, full and healthy then, had trembled as I pierced the open base of the "a" and worked the pin up through the second "o." I misjudged and the tip had stabbed the fleshy pad of my thumb, staining the southern Rockies red.

That was so long ago. I can't remember the first states very clearly, now. I only remember stabbing through each name once I'd reached the center. I must have been somewhere outside Columbus when Ohio's yellow-topped pin went in, but what makes Columbus stand apart from Buffalo or Kansas City? I am sure the waitresses there had dark circles, too.

Deep, controlled breaths to stave off dizziness. I cannot afford the buzzing, I cannot afford the lapsing. Tires crunch, and I merge back onto the highway. Black tar and metal signs. The road makes sense. Remain between the painted boundaries, cascade forward like water in a pipe, be steady and only end by choice. There is always another curve, exit, or intersection. There is always a choice.

§

I coast into a random town, stop and go, stop and go slowly through its blocks. Shoe repair shop, five-and-dime store. Ice cream parlor, old-fashioned barber. It is another era. I pet my car's dashboard. "You're more than a vehicle, know that? You time travel…time machine. This isn't now. Can't be, it's some yesterday before me. But I'm here, that's the thing about it. We're here. The same."

In the town square, a cobblestone roundabout lassoes a circular fountain flanked in benches. Blurred discs of copper and silver glint against the fountain's floor like stars and moons punctuating a foreign sky. So many drowned constellations. My foot unflexes and the time machine sputters to a halt in the present moment. I am out, I am moving toward the water and its sunken treasures. A fountain, nothing more, stark in its ornamentation and hardly fit for wishing. I pity its inner workings, the hidden pipes and pump. I ache for the smooth granite, how mute it is, helpless to protest the burden of mankind's desires. It is a wishing fountain only in its spitting wish to be rid of this onus, it burbles and we hear consent where none exists. Invade it, pelt it with the jangling contents of our pockets.

"Miss!" a voice calls, with a waver and hitch. That voice, a roller-coaster car cresting the highest hill, all rusty chains and wooden track. "Miss, you can't do that, get on out of there!"

There is a haunted feel to my shoes, perched on the fountain's brim. To look at them is to stare down desertion. Like the hollow shells of hermit crabs they speak not of the shell which is there, but the inhabitant who is not. The outlines of my feet vibrate below the water's surface. Two crabs, the spider's liquid cousins, crawl beneath me. So I turn away from the shoes and step gently, I speak gently, "It's okay."

"That money goes to charity," the second voice, hitch and waver, calls. It comes from a man whose face is melting with the decades, his age the flame atop a tapered candle. "I have half a mind to phone the police."

More quietly, I repeat, "It's okay," pinching coins up with my claws and drying them against my cotton shell.

How does the bearer of such a coin price his dream? From penny to quarter, four options—Lincoln, Jefferson, Roosevelt, Washington. Is his wish worth a single cent and emancipation, or five cents and an independent nation? Ten cents and the Depression's demise, or twenty-five cents and a fallen cherry tree, our American lie of the man who told no lies? How little it matters. Matter to atom, atom to element, element to alloy, alloy to screaming metal.

"Those are folks' wishes, miss. It's bad luck, what you're doing there."

But dreams aren't forged in metal. I could tell him this, that wishes don't live in nickels and dimes, but skin cells. Before the toss and tiny splash, the wisher frisks his thumb, slick with desirous sweat, across the coin. Bits of his fingerprint, his identity, his being, flake away. His own dead cells crust a dead president's chiseled visage. His cells wash into the water, become one with it, enter the dance of hydrogen and oxygen, those atoms fused into molecules. In summer heat the tempo quickens, fast and delirious. A moment of agony, and tangoing molecular partners slip far from one another, turn to vapor. Our wishes turn to tired steam. Congeal miles above the earth, grow soft and amorphous. Turn to clouds that are the playthings of distant imaginations—there's a bunny a Komodo dragon a bridge a mushroom a basketball player mid-leap.

It doesn't matter where the dreamer drowns his coin, that isn't where the wish is made. Rain falls, a thousand miles down a dark highway, and it is where the single cell-laced droplet splinters against the scalding asphalt that any dream is truly made or broken.

Rivulets run down my fibrous limbs and the cuffs of my pants grow dark and heavy. A fit of coughing, forced up my throat and through my sinuses. "Word association, I say cough, you say illness." No reply, on I go. "Illness to mutiny, mutiny to ships, ships to pirates, pirates to thieves, thieves to..." The minutes pass and I cannot articulate the vibrating desperate thing crawling through my gut.

§

The motel is a rundown L-shape. I take a space in the gravel lot nestled in the building's inner angle. Cargo pockets stuffed with singles from the passenger seat and glove box, I zip the map into my duffel and head for the office. My foot catches a lifted fracture in the front walk. A line of splitting, scorching pain erupts in my left hand as it meets the sidewalk. I gasp and roll onto my back, lifting my arm into vision, a slender white silhouette against the darkened sky. A shard of glass is planted in the exact center of my palm, curved and transparent green. The fresh wound is a smiling mouth, painted red, cavernous, devouring a sharp treat. Its crimson saliva runs along each side of the glass, converging at the point before dripping onto my cheekbone. My hand trembles violently as the flow increases, spattering dark drops across my collarbones and eyelids. War paint.

Clench teeth, grab, pull. Before it can speak. I throw my body forward and rock on my haunches. Heat and thirst and sickness grab me within and push out, I am dry heaving knives. A wail forms in my lower back, gathering barbs and sandpaper and rusty nails before pouring out of my mouth. A pool of blood rests in my cupped hand. I drink it. I mop my face and neck with a stray sock pulled from my duffel, smother the grinning hand with the sock.

Stable breaths, and I am on my feet, left hand a throbbing testament to my pulse, shoved in my pocket. Hidden. I lift the duffel, take the last steps, and plow through the office door. My voice is hoarse and strained. "I need a room."

The man at the desk has little hair, hooded eyes and a baggy theme-park souvenir T-shirt. He pushes aside a tiny black and white television and looks at me. His body instinctually shifts, tightening the jaw, squaring the shoulders, readying itself. Over my poisoned arm and the echoing depths of my stomach, I contemplate the man. The man looking disturbed, the man evaluating my features too closely. Like he has never seen a warrior or a spider. But I want a corner-tucked bed and a sink, and I offer no explanation. I won't be the one to teach him.

He glances at the wall for several moments, then turns back to me. "Got a credit card?"

My head rattles no back and forth. "I have cash." I stumble and close the distance between the man and myself. "It's right here, all of it, it's enough, counted in the car and it's as much as your sign says and everything, here." I plunge my right hand into my cargos, extract the crumpled singles, and spread them across the counter.

The man collects the bills, attempts to smooth them and form a stack. His motions and words are lost in the gray and black dots framing my vision, the cigarettes putting themselves out against my eardrums. A world of hot ash. But he holds out a key now. I grab it and bolt.

It had to be glass. I could have rent my flesh upon a ridged rock or a twisted aluminum can, an open switchblade fallen from some patron's pocket. But it was glass. Green glass. Red blood. This communion of complementary colors horrifies me, but it's been done.

Not safe, not in this blackness. I sprint past numbered doors and stop at 207. My key works, and I am inside a bedroom for the first time in weeks, shuffling forward on my knees. My torso collapses on the bed, it smells of fabric and stuffing and laundry soap. Too many nights curled up with dust and ancient chip crumbs on my car's bench seat, windows cracked for ventilation, tucked away in the corner of a rest stop, beyond the rows of slumbering semis.

I rinse the wound out in the bathroom, gently scrubbing its edges with the tiny bar of complimentary soap. It gapes mockingly. I am so scared of it, so scared of the glass and the things in this world that break glass and leave it there for others to fall upon. I dash from the bathroom, past the bed to the motel room's door, groping at the swing lock and deadbolt to still my heart, returning mere beats later in the same panic.

The spidery appendage at the end of my arm needs stitches. I stabbed a daddy-longlegs with a straight pin when I was little. He spun like a pinwheel, his legs, thin as eyelashes, clawed the hardwood floor in a futile attempt to escape the rod piercing his little brown center in place. My own fingers sit motionless, no final throes. Damaged nerves and blood loss can cause immobility. I squeeze the edges of the rupture together and apply a folded motel washcloth to my palm, closing my fingers around the makeshift dressing. I keep a roll of duct tape in my duffel. It repairs clothing, furniture, vehicles. People. I run the tape around and around my fist, binding it.

I know turning on the television is a mistake even as I do it. It is the center of all things ugly and that is the last of what I need. I turn it on. There's blood. Change channels, there's a tanned midriff, hip, thigh. Change channels, there's a midsize sedan. Change channels, there's a commercial for an all-natural cleanser. When I think about nature, when I think about cleanliness, orange film in a plastic tub is not what I think. Change channels, there's—

No. Nothing makes sense even as I make sense of it, if I ever do. It is possible to take a picture, but there's no truth in a frozen, stolen image. No truth in cherry trees and hatchets. I was younger once. My cheeks held color and fat. I even smiled. But there was a skeleton waiting to be born underneath and the smile was always a frozen, stolen lie. There's a girl on the TV screen, in one permanent fiction and another, another, and there are the evergreens of Colorado. There is its air, thinned by altitude, too thin to breathe. Too thin to carry my voice, my name, the capacity to heal.

It's funny when the words flash on the screen telling some puppet world that a person by my name is missing. The waitresses always have nametags and even if I know nothing else, I know their names. Mine no longer matters. It was forced to unravel itself. But Florida—I thought I might find safety there. I meant to touch its air, so thick and balmy nobody is left alone. Nobody has to hide. The air hasn't worked anywhere else. Florida could have held me. It's funny that it can't happen.

The salty winds and heat storms of Florida lick my mind. Tears and laughter and the difference is gone. It's been months. Something goes wrong in my chest. Months, and only now do I know that anyone knew. They never saw that I was missing when I truly was. I wish I was back in my car, navigating time and space, I wish I had a plateful of scrambled eggs to leave untouched and vending machine candy to leave unopened.

This boy died, they say it was a spider-bite. That was years ago. I barely knew him. But I knew a spider would get me someday.

The television is talking about diseases and disorders now. All mental things. The television is talking about danger and symptoms. Labels are nice excuses, I think. "Word association, excuses…leads to excuse me, excuse me to thanks, thanks to you're welcome, welcome to please, please to pleas no 'e,' pleas to begging, begging to gypsies, gypsies to pickpockets, pickpockets to thieves, thieves to…" I howl at the blood on the comforter because the picture it has painted is ugly.

The girl on the television is pretty. Her crinkled black hair, her wide, dark eyes. In front of a log cabin in Colorado she looks so pretty. And the television repeats that she is missing. I want to hurt her. Who would leave that? But I think maybe she was so pretty that someone decided to take her. Someone crept into her room one night on eight white legs and stole her. Thief. A man-spider wrapped her and bit her.

Now she is somewhere else. She cannot eat and she cannot keep the hot water in her head. She tries to find her way home but the air tells her she is wrong. If air is everywhere, how can she escape?

My eyes pour for the girl on the TV screen. I want there to be a point to the siren wailing outside this motel room, to the red and blue lights flashing in the gravel lot. But all I can think is how red and blue do not make purple. They are supposed to make purple. My chest goes wrong again. And again. Has my heart forgotten? If I follow the tides in Florida, it will remember how to beat.

I see myself made of salt and pepper, eggs and money, glass and pavement, lines in white and yellow, copper and silver, red and blue. And if a camera captures me this way, I will be so true, and my truth will be permanent. The light in Florida will reveal all of this, I'm sure. And I'll breathe its low air, inhale the ocean, vaporized.

"Vapor to air, air to cloud, cloud to mountain, mountain to peak, peak to point..."

But there will be no point. I smile for Florida, now. I will go there—I will—and the knocking on my door will stop. That knocking, without a point. The saltwater will scald the ridges and whorls from my fingertips and dissolve me into single cells, writhing at the heart of a hurricane.

My cells, just a handful of deserted wishes in the anonymous, sluicing chaos.

ACKNOWLEDGMENTS

It would take far too many pages to thank each individual who had a hand in this anthology. While we can't possibly thank everyone, we absolutely appreciate all of the people who made this book possible.

Thank you to all the writers who submitted a story for this anthology. The wide range of high-quality stories we had to choose from made selecting ten stories difficult. Without these talented authors, this book would not be possible.

Thank you to all of Columbus Creative Cooperative's dedicated members. It's fantastic to see so many writers supporting each other, supporting local literature and supporting CCC.

Most of all, thank you, reader. Your support of independent literature makes books like this one possible. With your continued readership, Columbus Creative Cooperative will go on to produce more anthologies, and writers everywhere will be inspired to write, improve and produce great stories.

AUTHOR BIOGRAPHIES

Aaron Behr continues to write despite his better judgement. He is always working on his next novel and short story. Like most artists, he is rarely understood or appreciated, but revels in it. This is his second publication through Columbus Creative Cooperative, the first was in *Triskaidekan*. An Ohio native, he and his wife Lisa live in Mount Vernon.

Read "June" on page 37

Chris Burnside is a playwright and professor at the University of Dayton, where he teaches courses on writing style, screenwriting, zombies and *Buffy the Vampire Slayer*. He lives in Hilliard with his wife and dog who (mostly) put up with his fascination with supernatural folklore. He would much rather write stories about ghosts and demons than believe in them, mostly because monsters are scary, and ignorance is bliss.

Read "The Screaming Bridge" on page 68

Ed Davis, a native of West Virginia, recently retired from teaching writing full-time at Sinclair Community College in Dayton, Ohio. He has also taught both fiction and poetry at the Antioch Writers' Workshop and is the author of the novels *I Was So Much Older Then* (Disc-Us Books, 2001) and *The Measure of Everything* (Plain View Press, 2005); four poetry chapbooks; and many published stories and poems in anthologies and journals. His full-length poetry collection *Time of the Light* was released in November, 2013 from Main Street Rag Press. West Virginia University Press released his novel *The Psalms of Israel Jones* in September, 2014. He lives with his wife in the village of Yellow Springs, Ohio, where he bikes, hikes and blogs mainly on literary topics. Please visit him at www.davised.com.

Read "Cracked Blacktop" on page 21

Emily Hitchcock served as an editor for this work. Find her complete biography on page 135.

Read "Billy White's Dog" on page 97

Anne Marie Lutz is the author of the fantasy novel *Color Mage* and its sequel, *Sword of Jashan*. She has also contributed to the *LocoThology 2013* anthology with a short story set in space. Anne Marie lives in Central Ohio. You can follow her on Twitter (@color_mage) or on her blog at annemariesblog.wordpress.com.

Read "The Summer of Growing Up" on page 85

Alice G. Otto is currently pursuing an MFA at the University of Arkansas, where she has received the Walton Family Foundation Fellowship in fiction and the Carolyn F. Walton Cole Fellowship in poetry, among other honors. In 2014 the Arkansas Arts Council granted Alice an Individual Artist Fellowship for short story writing. Her work has appeared or is forthcoming in publications including *Post Road*, *Yalobusha Review*, *Harpur Palate* and *Best of Ohio Short Stories*.

Read "Shadow of the Spider" on page 118

Brad Pauquette served as an editor for this work. He can be found online at www.BradPauquette.com, or see his complete biography on page 135.

Read "Road Crew" on page 11

Wayne Rapp has been a professional writer and film/video producer since leaving the University of Arizona with a degree in English. He has written two books, *Celebrating, Honoring, and Valuing Rich Traditions: The History of the Ohio Appalachian Arts Program* for the Ohio Arts Council and *Drawn to the Living Water: Twenty Years of Spiritual Discovery* for The Spirituality Network. His collection of short stories, *Burnt Sienna*, was a finalist for the Miguel Mármol Award. A short story, "In the Time of Marvel and Confusion," was nominated for a Pushcart Prize. His creative writing has twice been honored with Individual Artist Excellence Awards from the Ohio Arts Council.

Read "Rendezvous in Grass Valley" on page 105

Ralph Uttaro holds a law degree from Duke University and has spent the past thirty years developing real estate for a large regional supermarket chain. Born and raised in Brooklyn, he currently lives with his wife Pamela outside of Rochester, New York. His work has appeared most recently in *Bartleby Snopes*, *Toasted Cheese* and *decomP magazinE*. His stories have twice been nominated for the *storySouth* Million Writers Award.

Read "Denial" on page 54

Noell Wolfgram Evans has written a number of fiction and non-fiction pieces including the books *We Are Not All Winners* and *Animators of Film and Television*. As a playwright, his work has been produced across the country—from a theater stage in New York City to an elevator in Kentucky. A two-time winner of the Thurber Treat Award for Humor Writing, he's also written for the award winning short films "There Will Be Blocks" and "Faceless." He is currently working on a better version of this bio.

Read "Going South" on page 3

EDITOR BIOGRAPHIES

Brad Pauquette is the director of Columbus Creative Cooperative, which is a volunteer position, as well as the CEO and lead consultant of Columbus Publishing Lab (www.ColumbusPublishingLab.com). He is also the owner of Columbus Press (www.ColumbusPressBooks.com), an independent publisher of exceptional fiction and narrative non-fiction.

Brad's books *Sejal: The Walk for Water* (2013) and *The Self-Publishing Handbook* (2014) are available from all major retailers.

Brad is happily married to his wife, Melissa, with whom he has three sons. They live in an inner-city neighborhood in Columbus, Ohio where they strive to be good neighbors.

Find more information about Brad and his published work at
www.BradPauquette.com.

Emily Hitchcock is the Deputy Director of Columbus Creative Cooperative, which is a volunteer position. She works as a project manager and editor for Columbus Publishing Lab, a publishing services provider for author-publishers and small presses.

Emily lives in Olde Towne East, an eclectic neighborhood on the near east side of Columbus, where she keeps company with librarians, stray cats and other interesting characters.

ABOUT
COLUMBUS CREATIVE COOPERATIVE

Founded in 2010, Columbus Creative Cooperative is a group of writers and creative individuals who collaborate for self-improvement and collective publication.

Based in Columbus, Ohio, the group's mission is to promote the talent of local writers and artists, helping one another turn our efforts into mutually profitable enterprises.

The organization's first goal is to provide a network for honest peer feedback and collaboration for writers in the Central Ohio area. Writers of all skill levels and backgrounds are invited to attend the group's writers' workshops and other events. Writers can also find lots of resources and contructive feedback at www.ColumbusCoop.org.

The organization's second goal is to print the best work produced in the region.

The cooperative relies on the support and participation of readers, writers and local businesses in order to function.

Columbus Creative Cooperative is not a non-profit organization, but in many cases, it functions as one. As best as possible, the proceeds from the printed anthologies are distributed directly to the writers and artists who produce the content.

For more information about Columbus Creative Cooperative,
please visit **ColumbusCoop.org**.

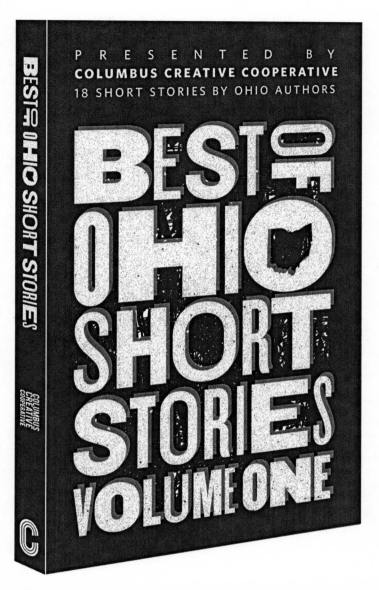

BEST OF OHIO SHORT STORIES

Volume 1

Find more information at
www.ColumbusCoop.org

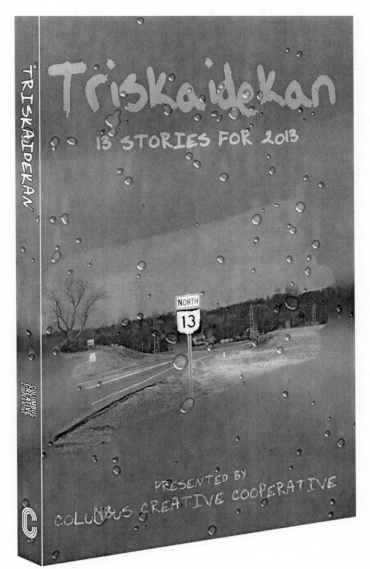

TRISKAIDEKAN
13 Stories for 2013

Find more information at
www.ColumbusCoop.org

Design and production servies
generously provided by

COLUMBUS
PUBLISHING
LAB

Complete Publishing Solutions for
Self-Publishers and Small Presses.

Editing. Design. Printing. Distribution.

www.ColumbusPublishingLab.com

Proudly based in Columbus, Ohio.

CPSIA information can be obtained
at www.ICGtesting.com
Printed in the USA
FFOW05n1632011214

9 781633 370173